Our Lives

Our Lives

Girls' and Women's Stories Across Two Millennia

John Connolly

iUniverse LLC
Bloomington

OUR LIVES
GIRLS' AND WOMEN'S STORIES ACROSS TWO MILLENNIA

iUniverse books may be ordered through booksellers or by contacting:

iUniverse LLC
1663 Liberty Drive
Bloomington, IN 47403
www.iuniverse.com
1-800-Authors (1-800-288-4677)

Because of the dynamic nature of the Internet, any web addresses or links contained in this book may have changed since publication and may no longer be valid. The views expressed in this work are solely those of the author and do not necessarily reflect the views of the publisher, and the publisher hereby disclaims any responsibility for them.

Any people depicted in stock imagery provided by Thinkstock are models, and such images are being used for illustrative purposes only. Certain stock imagery © Thinkstock.

ISBN: 978-1-4917-2773-7 (sc)
ISBN: 978-1-4917-2774-4 (e)

Library of Congress Control Number: 2014904830

Printed in the United States of America.

iUniverse rev. date: 03/19/2014

CONTENTS

For my parents, Helen and Joe Connolly, who taught us to seek truth.

FOREWORD

The tradition of all dead generations weighs like a nightmare on the brains of the living.

—Karl Marx

History doesn't repeat itself, but it rhymes.

—Mark Twain

Of these two quotes about history, the one that best describes the relationship between the girls and women whose stories make up this book and the lived experience of girls and women in ancient China, Pompeii, or on the Great Plains is Marx's. The stories presented here are meant to represent how girls and women lived in different periods and, thus, in very specific circumstances. To use a word from social psychology, they were conditioned by the world into which they were born—a world that had a complete and total understanding of how girls and women were supposed to believe and behave. Even had they doubts about the actions of a king, emperor, elder, priest, or imam, neither Zhang, Shi, Fatima, Natalya, nor Hoski would, as we would, question the political or religious order in which she lived. Most of these women were illiterate, and none had ever voted; indeed, it is likely that only Natalya had ever heard of voting. Again, with the possible exception of Natalya, who lived during the last third of the 19th century (and could have lived into the twentieth century), none of the women in this book imagined a future for their children that was significantly different from the life they led.

This was not a failing of their imaginations, of course. Rather, what we understand as the possibilities of life—whether to become a doctor, go to law school, or choose to remain in the home and raise one's family—would have been baffling to Hoski, Adjoa, and even Anne. Their roles, like those of the men around them, were set out—for some even written in the stars—long before these women walked the earth. Like Zhang, they knew the broad outlines of history; in her case, the victory of the Sui Dynasty. But history was like a river, flowing toward them and extending far into the future.

Even as it brings a smile to one's lips, Mark Twain's quip about history rhyming signals how we tend to view the history we read. Unlike the girls and women depicted in this book, we believe that even given the restrictions society (and yes, history, in the form, for example, of laws or borders) imposes on us, we are (largely) free to make our own futures. When we view history, we see patterns or similarities across time and cultures.

For example, stories of girls and women who were separated by thousands of miles and years emphasize the importance of women's purity—or, to put it clearly, their virginity. Surely this tells us something about the very nature of social organization. None of the women written about here could choose their own husbands, though for different reasons. Yet all of them either hope that these men will treat them well or are thankful that they have. Similarly, the women here believed in the power of folk stories. Adjoa, Shi, and Devika would have been baffled by Natalya and Sofia's religion (they were Russian Orthodox), but these three women would have immediately understood the story Nadya told Natalya and Sofia.

These women are aware of politics and the doings of emperors and kings. But the fleeting glimpses of what historians often call "great men" are themselves telling. Like more than 90 per cent of the men who lived at the same times, these women are unable to affect the greater world around them. Gaia may strategize, but she is powerless to affect the Caesar in Rome.

It would be going too far, however, to say that the women are powerless. One of the common threads in these stories is the presence of what might be called their secret world, a world which men rarely enter and might scarcely imagine exists. It's not the world of the Portuguese slave ship captain who will load a human cargo one-third of which will likely die before being sold in the New World. It is not the world of Louis XIV, the king for whom *les filles du roi* are named. But on the level of women's day-to-day lives, what historians sometimes refer to as "lived experience," it was real, vital, and fulfilled these women's emotional and social needs. Who has a richer emotional life, the emperor or Shi? Between the two of them, who has a richer imagination?

The stories collected here illuminate, as the title says, girls' and women's stories, stories that traditionally have been left out completely or pushed to the margins of history. It is worth noting, however, that women's stories are not the only ones to be so treated. In a poem entitled "A Work Reads History" written in 1935, three years after Adolf Hitler became Chancellor of Germany, Bertolt Brecht wrote about others whose stories have not been heard.

> Young Alexander conquered India
> He alone?
> Caesar beat the Gauls.
> Was there not even a cook in his army?

His point and the point made by these stories is that history is still an all but untilled field. Anne's story sketches one woman's life, but what of the men who built the Ursuline convent?

Buried in the graveyards of the world, many mass and unmarked graves, and on streets and fields where bones have long turned to dust are tales of women, men, and children, each of whom had a voice, loved and was loved, hated and was envied. None are like the ancestors that peer down at Natalya, for none had their pictures painted or their memories preserved.

Yet each lived—that is, each walked the same earth we do, and each, if we listen carefully enough and learn to look beyond just the pomp of glorious history, has a story that we can learn from.

Nathan M. Greenfield

INTRODUCTION

Our Lives is a series of stories that provide pictures of struggle and strength in many different societies.

What makes history live? Stories about individuals who take us to places we have not been. They are a basic vehicle for conveying information about people, events, or beliefs. Before humans could write, we told stories, and we continue to do so.

The book is the product of eleven creative minds. Ten young women and men have opened up worlds of girls and women over nearly 2000 years, and their images have come to life through original sketches.

This initiative is the evolution of discussions about blending creative writing and accessible scholarship. It began as a conversation with a neighbour, Andrea Abbott, in Ottawa, Canada, who had participated in a creative writing initiative with many of the authors. Through social networks, I was able to communicate with all of them, located in a variety of countries.

Each writer was given a time frame and a contemporary country as reference points. For example, the young girl Hoski came to life as a character using the years 1350 to 1450 and the United States as the framework. Hoski's story, like all of the others, was the result of significant research about that time period and the development of a fictional character.

Melissa Aytenfisu's sketches flowed from her own research about each of the time periods and ideas and suggestions provided by each author.

A well-established Canadian historian, Nathan M. Greenfield, provided pertinent questions following each of the texts. They are valuable for teaching purposes in a secondary-school context and for the general reader who wants to reflect in greater detail about their content. He also wrote a thoughtful foreword.

Learning about the lives of girls and women over a lengthy period of time is intended to stimulate discussion about those lives as well as their counterparts today.

John Connolly

GAIA VALERIA

Sarah McKeagney

"Oh, I hate this pomp," Gaia Valeria muttered darkly, arms held aloft as she watched the bright fabric snake around her body. The morning sun drenched the courtyard, promising a scorching summer's day.

"But clothes say so much about a person," the slave girl said with a smile as she fixed the golden yellow dress with an ivory clasp and flattened the folds. She belted the *stola*, causing the young woman to squirm.

"Oh, of course they do, but must it be so *dull*, Lydia?" Gaia said, waving her arms around in exasperation. "Narcissus, who so loved himself, couldn't possibly have cared for his looks half as much as you care for mine."

"Perhaps, Mistress, but Narcissus wasn't the daughter of one of the wealthiest spice merchants in Pompeii. Let alone a dutiful wife and mother-to-be."

"Well, Narcissus certainly wasn't as pregnant as I am, I give you that," she commented drily, her bronze face curling into a frown.

Lydia bent to fix the weights in the hem of her mistress' tunic as Gaia gestured toward her chest of jewels. Another slave opened the wooden box, revealing an interior that gleamed even in the shade of the porch.

The maid's dark eyes fell onto the large bump of Gaia's abdomen. It made her look so young. "We all have our own struggles to face," she murmured softly.

"The gold bracelets today, with the pearls, Lydia."

Lydia did as she was told, lifting the golden trinkets onto outstretched wrists which the young lady regarded with a lazy contempt. Against the red and blues of the intricately painted walls, Gaia glowed in her golden attire.

"Did you know that all the ladies in Rome are fair-skinned? It's a symbol of status. They never have to go outside, if they choose not to. Crazy, isn't it?" Gaia barked a laugh before it died in her throat, hands falling to rest gently on her stomach. "Depriving themselves of simple pleasures like a sea breeze or . . ." She stilled, eyes fixed on her hands as a thought lay on the tip of her tongue.

Lydia waited.

"Apparently," Gaia began, her voice falling to little more than a murmur, "it's a girl." She paused, digesting the information. Eyes turned to gaze at the courtyard's water feature. "The midwife said that she swears it to be a girl."

Lydia silently shut the chest and moved around the young woman, dusting off her own tunic, a faded orange. "She is a midwife, not a soothsayer, my lady. Only the gods know what is to come."

Her nimble fingers tugged deftly at Gaia's dark curls, coaxing them into submission. "There's nothing that can be done."

There were things that could be done. Prayers could be said or spells cast; the women in the kitchens told her so. There were so many possibilities these days—ways to prevent a pregnancy, ways to be rid of the baby altogether.

Gaia nodded, accidentally tugging on her own hair with a wince. "You're right, of course," she said. "We'll just . . . have to wait and see, I suppose." Gaia added with a whine, "Though I half expect that I'll have mothered the child by the time you've finished preening my hair."

Lydia began pinning the woman's hair into ornate curls, a smile tugging at her lips. The day always started in this way.

Lydia would wake before the sun appeared, her duties as a slave beginning in the kitchen. When Gaia rose, some hours later, Lydia would help her bathe and dress as Gaia bemoaned her difficult life. When that was complete, Lydia alternated between working in the kitchen and doing exactly what the lady of the house wanted her to do. Her life was not her own, but she had never known differently.

There were two kinds of people in the world: those who were citizens of the Roman Empire and those who were not.

Gaia, on the other hand, got up to the noise of a busy city: wooden carts on cobblestones, the cries of sellers of chickens and spices, and the general clamour of too many bodies in small spaces. It was the sound of livelihood, and she was enthralled by it.

As a child, Lydia remembered spying on Gaia as she went to fetch water for the kitchens. Before her lessons, the girl would follow her father around asking questions—questions about spices, about distant lands.

She asked of her lessons and just about anything else that popped into her head. It was a good thing her father doted on her. Gaia had a curious mind, and as a result she was encouraged to become a learned woman. Or as learned as any lady could be.

They were of the same age, Lydia and Gaia, both raised in the Valerius household. Before they knew of concepts such as social class or propriety they were already friends.

"You know, I'd quite like to be an ornatrice," Lydia said openly, eyes trained on fixing her hair with ivory pins. "I like doing people's hair, and I'm getting better. You could recommend me to the fair ladies in Rome."

"Indeed?" Gaia laughed, turning to regard the sallow-skinned woman behind her. "And you would leave me, your loving mistress, to fix my own clothes? Really, Lydia, you would be so cruel?" But before Lydia could answer, footsteps rang across the courtyard, causing the slave's lips to seal. She continued with her duty in silence.

"I thought I heard you out here." From the atrium appeared a broad-shouldered man, his white toga gleaming in the shade, flanked by three attendants. Gaia beamed.

"I'm afraid you must be mistaken, as I would never be so loud." Gaia laughed as the man took her hands with his own calloused pair.

"Forgive me if I don't believe that," he said, admiring her outfit. "Your father was showing me the workings of the port where the ships that bring the spices come in. It's astounding."

She nodded keenly. "It certainly is. Sometimes I forget he is a man of business and more than just my father."

"He's being very kind to me," he assured her before saying, "Are you free now? Because I would very much like to see Pompeii, and your father's been so kind as to offer to give me a tour."

There was something about Quintus Marinus that Lydia did not like. He was certainly ambitious; that was obvious. It was a dogged ambition, and it made him seem aggressive, hungry.

He will take your father's wealth, Mistress, take what is rightfully yours. You mark my words. Lydia may have been a slave, but she was no idiot.

"Give me just a moment, and we can go immediately," Gaia said excitedly. "It's best to see the city before it gets too hot."

The girl had missed Pompeii during her time in Rome. Seat of the emperor, the city was a feast to the senses in its own right, but Gaia had never been able to shake the feeling of being foreign from her fine linen gowns.

Pompeii was a part of her, ingrained on the backs of her eyelids: the cry of the ocean on a stormy evening, the vibrant green of the farms on the mountain. It was something about how nature was on your doorstep, how the gods were more present in life's wonders. People in Pompeii laughed more. They weren't weighed down by every minute detail of life and how the world might interpret one's actions.

Quintus hesitated. "Are you certain it's all right for you to be walking? You're not feeling faint, are you?"

Gaia scowled. "Quintus Marinus, I am 15 years old and perfectly fine. As kind as it is that you worry so much, I can tell you for certain that I am healthy and the baby is healthy too." A slow smile crept onto her face. "I was talking to the midwife today."

"What did she say?"

"It's to be a winter baby."

"And the sex?"

Gaia faltered slightly, swallowing down a thickness in her throat. "Well, she's a midwife, not a fortune teller. She can't predict something like that." Laughter erupted from the man, brushing off the answer with ease. He placed his hands onto Gaia's front.

"I suppose not. But whatever the gods give us, he will be strong. I know it." Quintus winked coyly.

"Lydia! Would you like to join us?" Gaia asked abruptly, turning to Lydia as her attendant finished fastening a linen shawl around Gaia's head and shoulders, taken aback. "Escorting my dear husband around town."

"The lady of the house demands my presence as soon as I am finished tending to you, Mistress." Lydia ducked her head under Quintus' scrutinous gaze. He was a military man; one could see it in his posture. And it seemed Gaia's husband did not view slaves with the same compassion as did members of the Valerius household. "I can fetch another of the slaves to escort you, if the mistress wishes."

It was said that many preferred death to being captured by a legion of soldiers. Her mother had told Lydia that when she was little, before Lydia knew that her mother spoke with first-hand experience.

"Well, best not keep Mother waiting then," Gaia said, thanking Lydia with the bow of her head. "Send Antia to wait for me in the atrium."

"Yes, Mistress." And with that, Lydia was gone, across the courtyard and deep within the mazelike rooms of the villa.

"Your fondness for the slave girl is commendable," Quintus said before he kissed her gently. Gaia's smile did not reach her eyes.

Pompeii was a well-organized city even if it was not the most beautiful. A holiday destination, it was always loud, often smelly. It was that kind of place. Yet certainly it was a beautiful place to the practised eye, one that had explored every nook and cranny, that had sat up all night to watch ships glide their way into port. Like all good things, it required practice. Yet any enthusiasm Gaia once had for guiding her husband through her childhood home was gone.

Her mind was distracted. Gaia began to see children everywhere. Pendants swung from their slender necks, proclaiming their innocence as they learned and played. They knew nothing of what was to come for them.

There was something terrible about how closely linked life and death seemed to be. Children were born to fathers already dead from battle or disease. Women wept as their babies were born silent.

There is so much in store for you, my little child. It felt bizarre, talking to the infant.

A fluttering movement as the baby within her stirred. *If the midwife is right, then prepare yourself, child. There is so much expected of you.*

Perhaps there was comfort in talking to the baby, acknowledging that there was life inside her belly. Yet even as she thought it, fear gripped Gaia like a vicious creature.

If you're going to get along in this world, you need to hold on, all right? Pray that your mother is strong enough.

Childbirth frequently claimed a mother's life.

Pray that your father sees you as the treasure that you are.

She smiled as her mind flew to Lydia.

Pray for friends in unlikely places. And always keep well-fed slaves.

Gaia thought back to the conversation she had with her mother the night before she went off to Rome to meet the man she was to marry. Then he had been no more than a handsome stranger she remembered from a party she had attended when she was 12.

"You're beautiful, Gaia. You're smart, with a good demeanour." Her mother's words were cool, foreboding. "But never forget, child, above all else you are a woman, and you *must* know your place."

She didn't know what that meant until she started to see things she wasn't looking for. The forum was as chaotic and enchanting as she remembered it to be.

Ahead, men gathered around her father as if the gold flowed from his very fingertips, his smiling face masking the smugness that she had never quite seen before. They were men of all statuses: craftsmen, architects, brothel owners, and labourers. Their existence was never put into question by empty, stretching days of dressing and weaving.

People are going to make this hard for you. There are days that you will feel like a shepherd with no sheep, a ship without a crew, but I have read the poems of ladies who could outwit the most cunning of emperors. People will ignore you. Every time you say something, prepare for a knowing smile, because people will doubt you; your jewels will forever outshine what you have to say. But never forget that I will love you. Oddly enough, I think I already do.

Gaia flushed at the thoughts flowing through her, her heart beginning to hammer. They were recklessly honest and as quick flowing as water.

Evenings will be full of socializing and rest. When you're old enough, I'll tell you every poem and song I know, and you, in turn, will teach your own children. You'll run your own house someday, and people will compliment your fair skin, your beautiful scent, the way you play music or sing. But these things are costly. Every night before you sleep you'll put the sweat of sheep's wool on your face because it makes your skin look youthful.

She smiled at the madness women put themselves through to obtain beauty.

You'll wear jewels from countries you'll never see. You'll succumb to the pressures of the world, because above all else, you are a woman. And you're not to forget that.

At nights, sometimes, I feel like I could rebel. Divorce my husband and run my father's business. I could, you know, but my bravery

*fades with the rising sun, and I dress like I should and thank Juno
for delivering me into the hands of a loving husband.*

"Gaia?" She started when she heard her name, eyes turning to
focus on her husband, who was looking at her with concerned
eyes. "Are you all right?" he asked. "You look a bit red."

"I . . . oh, yes. I'm just a bit hot—you know, the sun." Excitement
surged through her as she watched her husband give her an
understanding smile before the thrill of her lie flickered and died.
Extinguished.

"Your body must be under great strain, my love. If you wish you
can stand under one of the canopies while your father and I take
a quick look around the forum. We won't be long." Several pairs
of eyes turned to regard her before she nodded, dismissed.

*Your husband, while not your patron, is to be listened to. He only does
things with your safety in mind, after all.*

The shade of the overhang was indeed a comfort to the dark-haired
woman, droplets of sweat gathering at the base of her neck beneath
her linen dress. She sighed deeply as her father's entourage bustled
after the two influential men.

Gaia had just turned to address her attendant when her eyes found
another lady whose hands were immersed in the pile of blood-red
fruit next to her. The merchant was tossing her a disgruntled
look, muttering something about slaves and sampling his wares.
Her hair was pulled into a decorative knot, and her stomach was
bulging beneath her coarse tunic.

"Diana?"

The woman looked up in surprise before a smile spread across her
face, her search for good apples ceasing so she could bow slightly

toward Gaia. "This is a surprise, Gaia Valeria. How are you? I heard about your marriage. It was big news around here—Gaius' daughter marrying a Roman. It was a scandal, my lady."

Gaia laughed at that. Roman tourists, regardless of status, were only appreciated by the locals for their exuberance to spend their wealth in the bustling city and nothing else.

"I think he's probably going to savour the wine from your husband's shop this evening. And he doesn't much like to drink alone." The woman cackled, shaking her head. The shopkeeper threw Gaia a curious glance, looking from her yellow dress to her companion's scruffy appearance.

"I mean no disrespect, my lady. It's just Romans—you know."

Gaia bit back her smile. Diana was a freed slave who once had worked in the Valerius home before she bought her freedom. It wasn't uncommon in Pompeii, the wealth of the city so vast. Nonetheless, an ex-slave speaking disrespectfully of someone of superior birth just wasn't done.

"Diana, you're pregnant," she said, changing the subject.

Diana heaved a sigh, nodding her head toward Gaia's own bump. "It looks like I'm not the only one. Have your knees started to hurt yet?"

Gaia shook her head. "I think mine's a girl." Gaia said before she could stop herself. It felt good to tell someone. Perhaps Diana would understand.

Diana's brow curled. She looked from Gaia's tense face and her stomach before she shrugged nonchalantly. "Better yours than mine, my lady."

Gaia frowned. "Why?"

"If yours is a girl, she'll get an education. She'll get a rich husband who will look after her. If mine's a girl, what prospects will she have? She'll look after the house the same way I cared for yours. And gods forbid she marries a man for love and has lots of babies with nothing to offer them."

Gaia's cheeks turned pink; she was taken aback.

"What's tedium to a woman who knows no hardship?" The freed slave asked rhetorically, her chin jutting out as Gaia smiled a wry smile and nodded.

"You're right." *Is there such a thing as no hardship in this life?*

Gaia turned when she heard her name being called once again, her husband's face appearing among the clamour of people. His cheeks were pink from exertion, eyes bright.

Pompeii had a way of capturing one's heart, its pockmarked skin hiding many things. Some of those secrets were beautiful, and yet often they were not. It did not matter.

The sun beat down onto the backs of sailors and merchants, whores and their children as if daring to answer her with a booming silence.

No, it said. *No, there is not.* In the distance, the great mountain was rumbling.

Discussion Questions

1) Why is it important that Gaia be dressed up?

2) What do you think comes after when Gaia says to her slave girl that Roman women are "Depriving themselves of simple pleasures like a sea breeze or . . ."?

3) How is Lydia's life different from Gaia's?

4) What kind of a man is Gaia's husband, Quintus Marinus? Do you think it is a love match?

5) This story takes place in the Roman port city of Pompeii. A few years after the events related here, Mount Vesuvius erupted. Look up what happened there on 24 August in AD 79.

THE STORY OF DEVIKA

Einat Fogel-Levin

As my life is coming to an end, I think of my dear friend Nabhitha and some of the stories that I told her as well as my final story.

10

I was walking to fetch water from the river with Mama and all the other women. Since it was such a hot day, we decided to cool off in the river and wash ourselves. I was happy, as I had felt sticky and sweaty. You know how hot it is at this time of the year. I told Mama, but she just laughed and said that I should stop being so afraid of everything.

I don't think I am scared of everything, Nabhitha. I think I am pretty brave. You remember that time when I decided to go see the funeral rituals with all the boys instead of cooking. I know you didn't tell anyone about it, but I think Faarooq, my eldest brother, knew. However, he didn't say anything to Mama and Papa. I know he didn't, as they would have punished me if they knew.

Since I was a child, I'd been taught girls are not allowed to participate in the ritual ceremonies. Apparently, because we are girls, we are impure. I also know Faarooq loves me, because he got his wife to help me finish cooking in time.

When I took off my sari and went into the river, I noticed the water around me looked different. I thought it was some kind of magic, some kind of trick. Then my sister Chahna looked and said, "Mama, Devika's water looks different!" Mama glanced away from her laundry, and then she and all the other women laughed and smiled. They began singing to me.

Mama pulled me out of the water, helped me dry off with her sari, and said, "You see, Devika, this is why you felt sweaty all morning. Come here and help me. You are no longer a child—you are now a real woman." I looked at Mama, and although I knew about these things, I wondered what it meant to be a real woman. Do you know, Nabhitha?

11

A year ago, I asked if you knew what it meant to be a real woman. I don't know if I have the answer yet, but I guess I will have to start acting like one soon.

I am about to get married, Nabhitha, and I am so afraid. I don't know anything about the man. His name his Kamadev, and he is twice my age. I hope that I can be a committed and obedient wife as the gods want me to be. I also hope that he will be good to me and that he is handsome. It was only a few days ago that my parents told me about the marriage. They said that it had been arranged by Papa's friend Kaamil as is the custom.

Kaamil looked to find the most suitable husband for me. He is from my caste, of course, so he is from a farmer's family just like mine. I think this is good, as it means that it will be easier for me to get used to the housework. Kaamil says that Kamadev's family is well respected in their village, which is only one day's walk from here. I am happy that I will remain close to the river, but I am upset at having to leave my family and friends. However, Mama says marriage is a beautiful ceremony full of purification and love.

My friend Tamali, who is already pregnant with her first baby, has returned to the village only once since she got married. She looked happy then and said that she was treated well by her mother-in-law. In any case, Kaamil and my parents think that it's a good match for me, and the priests confirmed that the stars approved of it as well. I am excited for my wedding day, when I will be anointed and painted with henna like I have seen the village women do to others so many times. I can't wait to wear my red sari and bracelets . . . I just hope that my new family will let me keep the dowry jewelry in my own box.

I remember when Faarooq got married, his wife Yadva brought many jewels, money, and precious stones with her. It really helped us, as that year's crops were horrible . . . Nabhitha, I wish to continue telling you about the wedding, but Mama is calling me to come and help her collect buffalo dung and pound it into flat cakes so that they can use it for cooking and warming up when it gets colder. I really hope that someone in Kamadev's family is doing the same thing now so that I stay warm when I move there.

11

That's it. All the ceremonies are done—now it's just him and me. He has been nice to me so far. But he did something last night . . . that hurt. A lot! I had heard other newlyweds talking about it, and still . . . I mean, I wore my open sari to bed. Then Kamadev came and lifted it up. He told me to be relaxed and keep still. I tried my best, but it was not easy. It was not pleasant at all, and it ended pretty quickly, but I wanted to cry.

When it was over, I saw that the bed sheets had tiny red marks on them. I knew I should be happy, as this proved my purity to my new village, but all I could think of was how tomorrow's laundry would be harder because of it. I thank the god Shiva daily that I have you here with me and that I am healthy and strong, and yet I can't help thinking how much easier it is to be a man sometimes.

17

I love my little girl Padma. She is so wise and sensitive to the world around her. Today, I was working with her and her older brother Gafur on the land. (Gafur is a little bit ill this week, so his father let me take him with me to help with the crops instead of leaving him with the men to lead the water buffalo.) We saw a wealthy group pass by our field. They looked like Brahmans on their way to the traditional Kunbah Mela festival on the Ganges.

I wish I could go there as well, but Kamadev and I both know very well that we simply cannot afford the trip right now—or ever, for that matter. In any case, Padma saw the entourage and asked me, "Mama, where are these people going? Can we go as well?" I explained that only certain people can afford such luxuries, but she looked deeply confused. I then told her about karma. Gafur knew what I was talking about, as he has already begun to learn the Vedas with his father, but he still listened.

I explained to Padma that there is a certain order in our world and that each of us is destined to a specific life according to the way we lived our previous one. I told her that we are trying to be as good as we can be so that the gods will grant us a life of a higher order in our next life.

Gafur looked at me and asked if he was bad in his previous life, as he is not in the higher castes. I didn't know what to tell him, but when I looked into his eyes . . . oh Nabhitha, he had the look of his older brother who passed away. I know I should not be sorry about his death, as he was too weak for this life and would only cause trouble to our family. My mother-in-law made her thoughts on this matter very clear when she found me crying in my room, holding his blanket tightly.

And yet, Nabhitha . . . he was my firstborn child. I thank the gods every day for having two healthy children, for having a house and a shelter, for having a husband who does not harm me, for having a mother-in-law who treats me well. And yet, Nabhitha . . . I cannot help but wonder what if. Since I was taught to believe in karma, I hugged Gafur and told him what Kamadev and I repeat every day before we go to sleep: *"Chakrabat paribartante sukhani cha dukhani cha"*—happiness and sorrow rotate like a wheel. Kamadev taught me this. "You were not bad, Gafur," I told him. "This is just the gods' way of forcing you to be even better next time."

24

I have given birth five more times since the last time we spoke, Nabhitha. I know it has been a while; I simply did not have the time. Look at me—how I have changed. Even the way I talk to you has changed. Giving birth so many times, losing two more children, taking care of the household after my mother-in-law's death, making sure that my husband has enough to eat, that my children are healthy and educated, not forgetting to do all the traditional rituals—these things change you.

I walked to the river today with Padma, Almas, and Rajani, my three beautiful daughters. I loved this time with them. Padma became a woman a week ago; she's growing up so quickly. Looking at her, I remembered how confused I was when Mama told me I had transformed into a real woman. I know what she meant.

Being a real woman means worrying constantly—worrying that your children might be born crippled or injured; worrying about the possibility of having no children at all; worrying about losing your children as I have experienced; worrying about finding a match for your daughter; worrying about not being able to send her off with enough dowry; worrying about this year's crops as your husband ages, gets ill, and becomes unable to plow the fields; worrying about being good enough to have a better life next time.

Soon enough, Padma will start worrying. Kamadev has already asked one of his friends to set her up. Hopefully we will find a match for her soon, but I don't want to send her away yet, although I know it is necessary. It is the circle of life.

Another circle of life is starting soon too. Gafur is now about to begin studying the Vedas with a guru. He is 11 years old, which is a bit old for starting this, but I believe it will be for the best. He was always shy and smart, my boy, but not one of the strongest. When the day approaches, I hope to find him a beautiful young woman who will be good to him. However, he is about to leave our home for the first time. Soon the house will be a lot quieter when he and Padma leave us. I am sad, but at the same time I am content to see them grow and develop. I will have two mouths less to feed but two fewer pairs of hands to work on the land.

I am already preparing for Gafur's departure. I will make him lentil daal tonight, which he likes, because we are fortunate to have the lentils. I already packed him a little bag with all his valuables, which are not very many—two pieces of fabric to wrap around his waist and hips (Kamadev even bought him a new decorated one as a gift), a nice knife, and a wooden bowl and spoon. That should be enough for the first weeks of his student life.

I must go put the daal for Gafur on the chulah. We shall meet again soon, Nabhitha.

26

We shall meet again soon, I said, but I guess life had different plans for us. I won't be able to tell you what happened three days ago. Kamadev was on his way to the field when he accidentally stepped on a poisonous snake. Vageesh, our young boy who was with him, says it was a huge snake. In any case, when Kamadev realised that he was bitten, he tried to stop the poison from going up his leg. He limped all the way back to the village.

The village women saw him from afar and shouted to me. I turned around, told Almas and Rajani to keep working, and ran toward my husband. It was a long run, and when I finally arrived, I saw that Kamadev's face was almost completely blue—as blue as the anklet I have been wearing since our marriage day. He was sweating from poison, shivering from fear. I sent Vageesh to call Aabha, the village medic. I looked into Kamadev's eyes, and we both knew that it was a wasted attempt to save our lives.

There is something peaceful about this ceremony of ours. You walk down the road leading to the fire while all the other men and women of the village look at you. Some of the women sing. My daughters walk by my side, and surprisingly, they don't look terrified. They look calm, peaceful. They know that through this ritual, I assure redemption and salvation not only for myself and Kamadev but also for our next seven generations.

They look a little bit proud, my daughters—proud of their mother, who expresses her deep devotion to her husband. They are scared of losing me, but meanwhile they are relieved, knowing that they will not have to take care of me as I become an old woman or, worse, a widow whose head is shaved and who is banned from all social and ritual activities.

I am glad that they are here with me. As always, they give me strength. Seeing my beautiful Padma all grown up, married, and pregnant means I have achieved something in this life. Now the time has come for me to move to the next ones.

I walk along the road that I know so very well, the road on which I have seen so many satis being held. I am blessed and purified now, so many ask for my prophecy. I see nothing, but still I tell them that they will be blessed, cured, and prosperous just as I was told so many times before.

I wish my mother could be by my side and help with my sacrifice. As this is not possible, the village's eldest woman is here, waiting to instruct and guide me into the fire.

For the first and last time in my life, I am the centre of attention.

I kiss my girls one last time. I smile and wave at my friends and family, some laughing and some crying. I look at my village one last time. The time has come to say goodbye to them and to you, Nabhitha.

The fire is close to me now, and the smoke is suffocating, but I am not worried for the first time in many years.

Discussion Questions

1) Why does Devika say that she and other girls are impure?

2) Why is it important to Devika that her friend Tamali tells her that her (Tamali's) mother-in-law treats her well?

3) Why are the bed sheets, which are stained with blood, shown to the village after Devika's first night with her husband?

4) Since Devika singles out the Brahmans going to a festival on the river Ganges, she must not be one. What was the social hierarchy in Devika's India?

THE DIARY OF ZHANG LIHUA IN THE YEAR 595

Brittany Hathaway

15th Day of the First Month

Today was a day of celebration in my city, Daxing. It is the Lantern Festival, and it's fairly new but is my favourite of all festivals. The streets are lined with beautiful, brightly coloured lanterns. However, the main attraction is the dancers and musicians at every street corner. My two sons are overjoyed at the performances. My youngest is particularly taken with a woman playing the pan pipes.

My husband, Zhang Wei, accompanied us along the Great North-South Street where the main festivities took place. Our household is in one of the gated wards in Northwestern Daxing, and it is not very often that I am able to see so much of the city. The walk gave us a wonderful view of the emperor's palace situated at the city's northernmost point.

While the palace is nearly 15 years old, the construction of the rest of the city is ongoing. I was surprised that as soon as we left the main streets we saw remnants of ancient dynasties right next to newly constructed Buddhist temples.

Perhaps the most interesting aspect of the Lantern Festival is that it shows the many different cultures here in the capital. I must remind myself that the Southern nobles who were brought from their defeated cities have only been living in the North for a few years. I have lived almost my whole life under the Sui Dynasty.

My city was conquered by the emperor when I was only five, and I have little memory of the Northern Qi Dynasty or its customs except for my parents' religion. The Chen Dynasty of the South was defeated only six years ago. The nobles and officials who came to the capital still hold onto their culture and speak in ways that are difficult to understand.

The Southern nobles brought with them their tea and rice which grows well in their provinces. Unfortunately, many of them look down on Northern ways. They view our literature and art as underdeveloped compared to the fancy language and style of their artists.

Although they were defeated by the emperor, most of the nobles around him have adopted the long, brightly coloured silk dress of the former Han Dynasty. The adaption of tribal Northerners, who once held the majority of power, to a Han Chinese way of life gives us a middle ground on which to meet. It is not always obvious on sight, the difference between North and South, but when an individual speaks it takes only a few seconds into a conversation to realize the cultural differences.

Overall, the music, sights, and bright colours of the lanterns greatly pleased me. My place as a woman is within the confines of our family home, and I have every comfort provided for me. However, I want to continue to see new things.

5th Day of the Third Month

I have great respect for and care deeply about my husband. However, his family forces strict Confucian values upon me that I find difficult to accept. The teachings of Confucius focus on guiding humans to be altruistic, ethical, and above all to know their place in society. Some concepts remain foreign to me, but I am trying to learn them.

My day begins with meditation. I rise early, and with the aid of my Buddhist prayer beads I slowly chant the mantra to empty my mind of idle thoughts. This is my favourite part of the day, because it is the only time that I truly own. Wei's family would like me to give up my Buddhist ways, but I cannot do that. They are deeply ingrained in me. And though I know as a wife I could never say this to Wei's parents, the fact that the emperor himself encourages Buddhism among his people means that they can push me only so far. The acceptance of and freedom from pain that the Buddha teaches has helped me survive being away from my own family.

Following meditation, my time immediately becomes devoted to my two sons, Lun and Qi, aged 3 and 6. I am fiercely proud and protective of them. That I have already given Wei two sons gives me a certain amount of respect in the household, as opposed to Wei's younger brother, who only has one daughter after four years of marriage. I must raise my children according to Confucian ideals. My role is to be a kind and loving mother and to encourage an unfailing loyalty to their father.

When I am not watching over my boys, I do manual labour in the home under the rule of Wei's mother, Zhang Na. Her word is law, and I know my place. If she wishes me to prepare a meal or clean a room, I do it. Thankfully, Na is kind and, I think, remembers what it was like to live under her mother-in-law's thumb. I worry sometimes that she might punish me because of my strong bond with Wei, but so far there is little jealousy about the attention that my husband pays to me.

We each come from a different Northern dynasty, yet our cooking styles are similar. Vegetables, meat, and grains are prepared in a stir-fry. Na trusts me with food preparation, but it was not always this way. There was one occasion when I took the buzzing of flies around a piece of beef too lightly and made the family violently ill. Na instructed me on the ways to check that food is fresh so that I would not make the same mistake again.

When I get some free time during the day, I turn to my books and writing. Wei's family does not understand why I want to learn to read and write. As followers of Confucian teachings, they believe that educating women is a waste of time. However, Wei's father became much more accepting of my love of reading and writing and even my Buddhist traditions when he saw that some of the books I read allowed me to better teach my sons the Confucian way.

Surprisingly, it was Wei, who is a scholar, who taught me to read and write. Indeed, my goal for this diary is to practice my writing. At first I found it difficult, but my writing skills have shown me the Confucian ways and allow me to keep my diary. After my sons, being able to read and write is the greatest gift my husband has ever given to me.

Once Wei returns from his duties in the evening, my time is dedicated to fulfilling his needs. He is never too demanding of me, but it is my responsibility to ensure that no task is left undone, such as cleaning up the wax from the candles burned for the ancestors. When night falls, it is time to retire with my husband and await the beginning of a new day.

20th Day of the Sixth Month

I am proud that my increased skills in reading and writing mean that I can help my husband. Doing this is not so unusual in Northern culture—after all, the emperor's wife contributes to her husband's decisions on a daily basis. But my ability to read has allowed me to learn much about my husband's work. I try to help when he is overloaded with things to read.

Wei works for the Board of Public Office, which appoints local officials in the various counties. Given that they have only been in place a few short years, they have made great progress in uniting the Sui dynasty after decades of division and war. One of their most important improvements is the Rule of Avoidance—no official can serve in his local area, and an official can only serve in one area for a maximum of three years. This helps to eliminate the practice of favouring relatives and friends from wealthy families.

At the lower level of the government, the results of the Civil Service Examination determine who gets a position. That was how my husband got his—that and the fact that his father held a key position in the ruling Northern Zhou Dynasty. However, within the upper echelon of power, known as the Three Departments and Six Ministries, almost everyone in power comes from the same region as the emperor, and many are related to him through blood or marriage. It is unlikely that Wei will ever achieve more power than he holds now—Confucianism is not highly respected among the emperor's men.

Perhaps this is an area in which I can advise my husband. The men of office that the emperor has chosen are much like my own father—traditional military leaders. Wei is often at odds with them. They have been shaped by the warring nature of the North and care little for Confucian values. Wei often returns home frustrated because he does not understand the men he works with. When we are alone, he sometimes asks me about military leaders, because I come from that background myself. I know I can never hold land or office, but at the very least I can help my husband accomplish his duties.

I heard a rumour that the emperor recognizes the need to separate himself from the military focus of these men. I think that in order to achieve peace, the dynasty must abandon the idea that the army and its leaders have total power. Changes are being made—this year, weapons were taken from the general population. The emperor has supported Confucian intellectuals by building schools focused on Classical teachings. I wonder how long this will last.

12th Day of the Eighth Month

There is one issue that has been bothering me lately, and that is my own ethnic identity—and that, I suppose, of the Sui Dynasty itself.

A Southern noble would probably see little difference between my culture and my husband's; to him, we are both Northern. But while Wei is a Han Chinese, my family originates from the Xianbei tribe. Clans from the Xianbei tribe once held power in the North, so large that it could take 100 days to walk across. The nobles of the Northern dynasties were primarily not Chinese. But in recent years, non-Chinese have made great efforts to conform to Han Chinese ways of living. Names have been changed, intermarriages are encouraged, and some customs have been dropped.

Yechang, the city where my family held power, fell to the Zhou Dynasty 15 years ago, and I left that culture behind. I know very little of Xianbei ways beyond the image of my father—the emphasis on military power, Buddhism, and only the basics of Classical education. If it were not for my dedication to my religion, people would see me as no different from the Han Chinese. Even that distinction is fading with the emperor's continued efforts to spread Buddhism. My father arranged my marriage to Wei so that I could learn the ways of the Han in order to adapt to the new dynasty. But at what cost?

There is little room for me to assert my own culture and beliefs in this household. I can pass on some Buddhist teachings to my sons but only when no one is watching. I have won some battles, such as my insistence on my husband having no other wives, although I am lucky that he still finds me pretty. But my curiosity and interest in my background are rejected outright. I am scarcely allowed to visit my own parents. Some days I feel torn in many directions, confused about my true loyalties. I must, however, uphold the traditions of my husband's family.

18th Day of the Twelfth Month

As the end of the year approaches, I find myself thinking about the changes that have happened in my life since I started this diary. My sons are almost a year older, a little stronger, and a small step closer to being men. I have grown closer to my husband. The emperor continues to bring changes to this newly formed dynasty.

This upcoming year I will be expected to produce another child. I cannot help but hope that it is a girl. It is the opposite of the wishes of my husband's family, but perhaps that is what makes the idea so exciting. My sons will have the world handed to them. As for my daughter, I would have to work hard to teach her how to survive in a society that will do her no favours.

I want the opportunity to do more, but I see little way to achieve this. I do not know how much further I can push my husband's family. Surely they would allow me to learn new skills, such as how to play the pan pipes that my son loves so much. After all, there are plenty of female musicians.

Discussion Questions

1) Today, we expect everyone to be able to write. Indeed, it is a good bet that everyone in your class texts or messages on such services as Facebook. Why, then, is it important that Zhang Lihua is keeping a diary? What might happen to her if her parents-in-law were to read it? Does she write anything that could get her into trouble?

2) The story corresponds to around the year AD 600. Do you think that a woman married to an official in the court of the French King Chlothar II (the Great, the Young) would be keeping a diary?

3) Zhang Lihua discusses two different religions: Confucianism and Buddhism. Does either emphasize—like Roman Catholicism, the religion that was dominant in Europe at the time—ideas about God, resurrection, and the afterlife? Does either have a heaven?

4) Why is it important that Zhuang Lihua bore her husband two sons?

5) The differences between the peoples who come from the North and those who come from the South are many. Cooking is one; dress is another. What are some of the other differences? Can you name differences between people who come from Canada's north and Canada's south? Are there differences between people who come from the northern United States and the southern United States?

EADBURG

Tyson Lowrie

I hope to make it to Southampton before I die. The wagon is almost here, and my fare is paid. I don't know how fast the wagon can travel and the horses pull. I only hope it's faster than the blood can pour out of my insides, coming out of my mouth when I cough. I also hope that Christ, Thor, and Woden do not come for me before I reach the city.

My husband is trying to strengthen me for the journey. He has given me not only extra ale in the past several days but also a few apples and plums and peas and fava beans in addition to the usual brown bread and barley porridge. Last night I even had that most precious treat, a mouthful of cheese. He could not spare any meat though; our pig is not yet ready to be slaughtered.

Hopefully the nourishment I have been given will be enough to get me to Southampton and back. In that town, they have the most expert healing methods of any that we know. They can draw the bad, excess blood out of me and give me the necessary herbs so that I might heal and live to be an older woman than my mother was when she passed. My husband, though, says I cannot spend too much on medical care, as it may well be a waste for me. Better to keep it for the living, he says, and those who will live longer, such as my children.

I do not know what a city looks like. They say Southampton is so large that it may contain thousands or even tens of thousands of people. When I was a girl my father used to tell me stories he'd heard, not of our ancestors, but of the Latin-speaking peoples whose old coins we sometimes wear as jewelry. He told me they had large cities not just here but across Britain and the lands beyond the water. But we hear that those cities are mostly empty.

Our hamlet is called Wesbury, not far from another small village, Wilton, in the kingdom people call Wessex. It's named for our ancestors, the Saxons, this being their westward kingdom. We are perhaps 200 people in our little community. I am told there are hamlets like ours scattered all about, but I have not seen many. My husband, who is still hale, visited Southampton once, trading some of his few coins, sciattas, to buy a few tools to bring back home. Now that I'm not strong enough for work because of the illness, the only use I can be is to travel to Southampton to trade for goods.

If I cannot come back, then my husband's brother will bring back whatever goods I can trade for. There is no question that we can acquire finer wares in Southampton than around us. Some of our neighbours think us crazy to send out a woman to travel; it hasn't been done in years. But this is one job I can still do. Ailing as I am, it does not take great health to sit in a wagon. Besides, there are still good roads that lead us toward Southampton. Other cities would require travel by river, and with all the stops I don't think I could muster the strength.

The hills around our village are emptier than they once were. My stepmother told me that we have had this land only since her marriage. My stepfather, her husband, used to scrape by on the hill nearby, farming the slopes like so many other families. The land was poor, so we have fewer people now in our hamlet than in my mother's time, and there were fewer in hers than my grandfather's.

Our world is getting smaller. The weeds, bushes, and wild plants are starting to swallow up the areas on the edge of our cluster of homes, on the hills and poor lands where once there were people who farmed them. My husband, who once travelled with our lord to fight, says it is like this everywhere. However, because of this we have better land than we once did, even though it's scattered about the village in different spots in case of a problem hitting one section. I don't know how much this is the case in other parts, but I'll be able to look out over the wagon as we pass through some of the countryside and see for myself.

I am telling you this, Cuthbert, so that you may know of our lives as you gather stories for the Bede about English history. Ever since I started to cough blood, I realized I will be joining my mother soon, and what I have will be lost forever. In the spring, my friend died, and a few of the girls whom I played with as a child 25 years ago have been dying. Others I know have already gone into the earth even earlier.

My mother passed on her knowledge to me before her death, and I am doing the same for my children. It is thanks to my mother that I have children to pass on to. Four of them have already died, but also thanks to my mother two are among the living. She told me to tie coriander to my thigh so I might have many children, and she was right, and so two have survived. She learned that medical knowledge from her own mother-in-law, a Celt, when she was just a young girl.

I wish, Cuthbert, that I could tell you more about the stories my mother and stepmother would tell me about our ancestors who took over these territories and drove out some of the raiders, subduing and marrying the rest. However, many of those stories are lost now, and the strange letters, runes, that even my mother and father had some knowledge of are completely alien to me. Nowadays, those who can read or write mostly use the script of the Latins. I can recognize a few words in that alphabet, as can my husband, but reading is best left to the religious men and the lords. You don't need the alphabet to plant barley or to brew ale.

As I tell you this story, my husband is in the fields, tending the barley and pruning some of the vines and weeds around the half of our fields that lie fallow. I have been too sick this past while to do some of the most basic tasks. In a couple months, when we harvest the barley, I'm worried I won't even be able to make ale, and our crops might spoil. I can only do the essential task of weaving cloth. No woman would be worth her weight if she did not weave cloth. I was once the best weaver in our village and made my husband proud. He sometimes even had a bit extra to sell for a few sciattas, if there were any in men's hands, or for some extra grain.

I have never been so far as Southampton, but when my husband came back he was full of stories of an incredible city buzzing with craftmakers. He also had tools of quality we'd never seen, and I fell to my knees seeing that he had come back safely because of the extraordinary danger of crossing kingdoms on the old Roman roads. I thanked God and visited the monastery and then came back home and privately thanked the gods of my ancestors as well, Thor, Woden, and Frig.

The north, they say, has a kingdom that is rising slowly and will soon consume us all. I am sure you have heard this, but I would not know. I have not been more than 15 miles outside the village, and I have learned that many kings swing back and forth over our heads, but I never see any of them. Ours is currently named Aethelheard. It doesn't seem to matter. We have only loyalty to our village's lord, whose father my own father saw die in battle.

My father, it is said, knowing that it would be a dishonour to come home alive after seeing his lord perish, charged forward and killed an enemy before being speared himself and gave our family great honour. He died when he was nearing 40 with me having just married. My husband likewise passed along honour to our children when similarly in battle he put himself between his lord and the enemy, willing to sacrifice his own life rather than let his lord's blood be spilled. Fortunately, both came home alive, and for gratitude the lord let him pay nothing to use the grain mill that harvest.

These are stories which I hear, but daily life is far less interesting, Cuthbert. For us life is more a matter of sowing our grain, my husband working with his oxen to break up the ground and plant our seeds. We harvest, thresh the grain from the husks, repair, and mend. My husband will take care of the children while I am gone, but then he has always been good with the children, and those were responsibilities we shared. He also cooks fairly well, so if I die our family will continue to survive.

It is the smaller tasks I am worried about—the mending, the cleaning, the repairs, the help with the harvest, and the work around the house that will be the most difficult. Collecting salt is also important, and though for the last couple years my back has ached while I did it, that has been my role. There is little good in slaughtering an animal if you don't have enough salt to brine it in.

Neither is barley, even the six-row kind, or wheat, enough to live off. Who can eat nothing but porridge and ale all their lives? We rarely have meat or milk, and so pears, apples, nuts, and mushrooms are best collected by the women of the village.

It is hard to have to struggle for so much, to prune the vines that would otherwise eat up so much of our fields at the beginning of every spring, to drag our animals out in April and to prepare the soil until our hands bleed, to scrape by, such a measly life. We have buried four children which is not unusual, Cuthbert, but grim business nonetheless.

The winter is coming, and increasingly it does not look like I will see it, which may be a blessing. It will be bitterly cold and wet, and though my husband built our house well, supported by posts throughout with a thatched roof, water can trickle in and ice can form outside. In the winter I weave what cloth I can so that we stay warm. The winter sees us thresh our grain, build new cattle stalls and huts above the pits we have dug before the ground freezes. My husband tries to plant orchards and fruit vines when he can so that we might have a few apples or plums to eat.

The road ahead to Southampton will be hard. Our own land has great protections for women against the potential ravishments of men. In our realm, if a man harms a woman the law will harm him to a much greater extent than he hurt the woman, but I am not sure if this is the case everywhere we are going.

For my part, I know only that I am descended from Saxons and Celts. I know that what happens within the territory marked off by dams, our lord's land, affects me the most. Yes, he pays tributes to greater lords, who pay tribute to greater kings, and it is said that they are threatened now by an even greater rising power, Mercia.

I suppose this web of tributes is what men like your master, the Bede, call Englishness, and seek to tell us as a story of a people.

But beyond these dams, I don't really know what waits. I know best what happens in the walls of my house, between the posts of my home, which is no longer than five men lying flat lengthwise and three wide. This is the ground where my life takes place, here and on the hide of land we farm.

I have heard men (mostly men) say that it is our Englishness that holds our society together, but I think it is our local lord. More than our Englishness, too, what keeps us together is the water mill. I'm told that in generations past they weren't so blessed as to have one of these, and so our lord controls it now.

I still have part of the property that was my mother's dowry which she passed down to me. It includes a hand grain mill, which I have never had to use. Whenever I think of the difficulties we face, I think of my mother grinding the grain for hours on end by hand, and I think I don't have it so bad after all.

Travel, Cuthbert, is now more dangerous. They used to say, in the days of the Romans, that a Roman citizen could walk anywhere in the empire without fear of being assaulted. Now? Well, let's just say that isn't the case. The times my husband has left, I've thought he might not come back. It would have been a silly turn of events and an unfortunate death to mourn and to have to wait a year before I remarried. For my trip to Southampton, I'm leaving Monday, right after the Sabbath, though that is also dangerous. The thieves know that we may not work on Sundays, so they lie in wait on Monday for greater traffic.

For my husband's part, he seems less concerned about my safety on this trip than my fidelity. He has been listening to the Christian monks who set up monasteries and eat white bread while the rest of us chew on brown bread and porridge. A woman, he says, tends toward sin, and with ale and encouragement can be easily led to another man's bed.

Every harvest festival, while we women sing, dance, and even play instruments, he keeps his eyes on me. His uncle told him once that we women were not to be trusted at harvest festivals. Having memorized parts of Theodore's Code, he says if either of us sins we know what penance to do, but he seems to remember the women's punishments more than the men's. Under the influence of ale, wine, and (if we are tremendously lucky) even an occasional sip of mead, the men think we can't be trusted.

Thinking of the harvest festival will make me sad, as it seems less and less likely that I will see it. I have fond memories of the sowing festival—us women dancing and making comedy for the men, and men playing trumpets, lyres, and pipes and then going out to hunt wolves and sling stones at birds.

I do hope, Cuthbert, that when the Venerable Bede tells his story, he will include some of the stories of common people so that his English history does not simply become a story of dead kings. I don't envy his task. To tell the story of an entire isle and all the tribes of people over hundreds of years is a massive undertaking. As for me, mine is simpler. I simply wish to make it to Southampton and, God willing, back to my children and husband.

Discussion Questions

1) Eadburg is very ill and prays to both Christ and the Norse gods Thor and Woden. Today, people might pray to Christ or, if Muslim, ask for Mohammad's intervention. In either case, Christians, Jews, and Muslims all pray to the God of Abraham. How can Eadburg pray to both Christ and the Norse gods (who are not Christian)?

2) What does Eadburg mean when she says it is too early to slaughter the pig?

3) How does Eadburg feel about the fact that the land is slowly reclaiming the villages around her?

4) Why is Eadburg telling these stories to Cuthbert? At one point, she mentions "the Bede." Look up the Venerable Bede. See what he did and ask yourself how his life's work changed how history is recorded.

5) Eadburg is worried about the possibility of attacks on the road. What are the legal issues that she discusses?

SHI

Tyrel Stokes

Home

Chan Chan, Chimu Empire

12th moon, day 5, morning

Shi awoke gingerly to the break of dawn and the rustle of fishermen preparing their boats for the day's catch. She placed her right hand by the window and paused momentarily, catching the shimmer of light on the breezy ocean and the silhouettes of rugged fishermen, providers of the community.

She waved to the fishermen. Two of them, the oldest and strongest, put down their lines and bait and halted their day's work. The two men unlocked their vice-like grips from the rudimentary pails used to carry their supplies. They wiped the sweat from their brows and smiled hopefully at the girl, whom they called daughter and sister.

These supplies would not do them much good today. The normally cool ocean felt warm to the touch, the ocean breeze felt deprived of moisture, and lifeless fish were scattered on the beach. The measured waves slowly pummelled the fish carcasses, and the stench of death rose up from the beach into the village. This had been the trend in recent weeks, and the village's collective stomach was beginning to feel the consequences.

The fishermen's waves wished Shi good luck while their eyes grieved her parting from the family household. Their grief was overshadowed by a deep pride. Shi, their family member, was the first girl in recent memory to be called to the court of the king to be his personal tailor and weaver.

The whole village was talking about it. Shi, the daughter of a poor fisherman and a crippled weaver, was a prodigy. They said she could turn the dirtiest rug into a poncho fit to worship in and that she once took a worn loincloth and by her grace and skill transformed it into a large gauze depicting the majestic profile of a jaguar. All agreed Shi possessed an uncanny capacity to pay attention to detail and an artistic vision that produced immaculate images of men, birds, and beasts.

Shi finally broke eye contact with her oldest brother and father and turned her attention to her youngest brother and mother who were fast asleep in the corner.

She stepped quietly out of the room and away from the ocean where one of the king's servants, dressed modestly in a simple poncho and loincloth, was waiting. "The king wants to see you," said the stoic servant. Shi nodded respectfully as she exited her village in the mighty city of Chan Chan for the last time as a resident. She followed the sand path past the homes of friends and families that she had seen a thousand times and paused to soak in the community that marked the first 16 years of her life.

"Follow me and keep quiet," said the servant emotionlessly as they ascended sculpted steps, crossing the gates dividing the Chimu Palace from the outside world. The walls towered over Shi, perhaps 10 times her stature.

Exquisitely sculpted friezes of fishermen wielding nets upon nets of fish jutted prominently out of the foundations. Each fish was perhaps one-quarter Shi's weight, each scale worth enormous amounts of energy and time.

But neither the walls nor their decorations affected her as much as the labyrinth of tunnels and narrow passageways standing before her and leading to the heart of Chimu civilization.

The servant's strict tone and her cold body language reinforced what was already apparent after barely a few seconds inside the lavish palace: Shi did not belong here.

As the servant guided Shi through the tunnels and passageways, she caught glimpses of the new world before her. She passed large storage rooms full of crops and men busy stacking them.

She passed sacred worship rooms lined with beautiful rugs, pots, gold-plated ornaments, and jewellery depicting gods and holy beasts. Upon the floors in simple but elegant robes, a handful of holy men and women sat crossed-legged worshipping, engaged in ceremony and scripture.

She passed busy offices full of bureaucrats. As she stared, the servant caught her eye and told her that these individuals were responsible for planning the building and maintenance of canals, what crops to grow, which communities should grow them, and the trade economy of textiles and other precious goods between the various Chimu tribes and communities. These men, only metres away, were the same faceless authority figures whom her father and brother worked for twice a year building canals.

As the pair snaked closer to the heart of the palace, the designs upon the walls became more elaborate, and the sharp echo of busy workers and worshippers softened until the hallways were filled with a dead silence.

Shi's heart began to pound loudly.

The servant walked briskly to the end of the hallway, turned around slowly, and whispered, "Wait here." Then she disappeared into the king's plaza.

A glance inward revealed the plaza to be more immense and more densely populated than the stillness suggested. In perfect file and order, Shi saw what seemed like about 100 priests, servants, and court attendants in two distinct groups. The ends of the two groups curled toward each other around the back of the ceremonial altar in the shape of a crescent moon.

Shi sensed tension spread throughout the plaza, seemingly crawling up the spines of holy men and advisors alike, making them very rigid.

The servant inched toward the very back of the plaza and the two men perched upon an elevated platform. The throng of onlookers made space for the servant's slender figure to approach the king and his high priest. As quickly as they parted, they reformed the half circle.

A short distance from the throne itself, the servant stopped dead in her tracks, graciously bowed, and then knelt before him, awaiting his acknowledgement. The king lifted his gold-laden fingers and bent his ear toward the high priest standing at his right. Behind the veil of his left hand, he whispered something quickly and then summoned the servant forward.

The king stayed put on his throne, and the high priest moved to meet the servant. Nodding mechanically and with eyes cast downward, the submissive servant listened attentively to every drawn-out syllable formed by the high priest's pursed lips. After a momentary stillness, a preoccupied king lifted but the end of his bejewelled index finger to dismiss her from his presence.

Slouched on his throne, eyebrows furrowed and eyes full of anxiety, the king did not resemble the omnipotent and fearless ruler about whom the villagers so often spoke. The king was not commanding; nor did his appearance resemble that of a god. Instead, a mortal-looking ruler sat staring distantly at the ceremonial altar. It was the look of a disturbed and anxious man.

In the darkest corner of the palace, Shi was shown to a crude working space. A spindle and loom dominated the centre of the room. There was also a small desk to keep her things tidy, stockpiles of cotton and wool, sacks full of natural dyes, and a small concave groove in one wall, presumably for her to sleep in.

"You have until the break of dawn. You are to design a wall piece for the king's chamber adorned with his side profile. The rest is up to you. You may use any of the materials in this room in the fashion that you choose." The servant nodded and then turned back into the labyrinth of hallways with an air of finality.

Impulsively, Shi produced a sound that was somewhere between asking the servant a question and begging her to stay.

The servant reluctantly stepped back through the entrance to the door. "Was that . . ." Shi paused, searching for the proper phrasing, but formality was not necessary.

"Normal?" the servant interjected.

"Yes," she whispered, caught off guard by the meek servant's openness.

"Is it normal that the irrigation canals run dry? Is it normal that the cool ocean feels hot to the touch? Is it normal that the beaches are covered not by sand but by fish?"

Shi shook her head, tears slowly flooding her eyes.

As she turned to leave again, Shi's hand rose to catch her attention and ask another question, but the servant already knew what she meant.

"When?" the servant blurted out. The desperation in her voice betrayed the coldness in her face. "We find out tomorrow." She left the room, leaving Shi trapped inside a void of emptiness.

Her mind raced frantically. The servant's cryptic tone was clearer than ever. The silence in the king's court, his complexion, and the demeanour of the servant were but three different shades of fear, three different ways of asking the same question: "Do the gods require a sacrifice?"

Distraught and full of apprehension, Shi's head conjured up graphic images from her childhood and the last time the word *sacrifice* had been part of the community's vocabulary. Shi had been 6 years old as her youngest brother was now.

She remembered vividly the mass grave dug and filled with the criss-crossed bodies of well over 40 children. She was the same age as the other children; only her good fortune and 70 llamas had saved her from the same fate. The images of that day were still so clear: children placed delicately at right angles atop llamas, llamas atop children, each intimately placed in its proper spot as part of the sacrificial ritual.

Only she didn't remember them as bodies. "They're patterns, just strings lying in an intricate pattern like a quilt for the gods to see," her mother had said. "It makes the gods happy."

She snapped herself out of a dream. Her nimble fingers, which were no longer trembling, fumbled through wools and cottons of various spins and thicknesses. They rested upon fine alpaca wool and a set of rustic clay dyes and natural earth tones. The duo seemed to marry durability with a subtle sense of elegance and nobility fit for a monarch.

Despite the productivity and eagerness in her fingers, however, she was unable to proceed.

In her mind's eye, she saw not the majestic profile of the most powerful being in all of Chan Chan, in all of the Chimu Empire, but just a man in a chair.

Finally, she set to work. Minutes manoeuvring the fine threads in and around each other turned into hours coordinating the overarching patterns and themes of the wall piece. From the microscopic to the macroscopic, the wall piece was slowly assuming its shape. The dual nature of a single thread, the way a single thread is both structurally integral and aesthetically meaningless to the textile as a whole had always fascinated Shi.

Shi felt that in a way she and her family and friends were much like strings. They caught the fish, grew the food, spun the wool and made the clothes. Individually, they were invisible, but collectively they were the backbone of the community.

Staring into a half-woven approximation of what was to become the king's forehead, Shi wondered if the king felt like a string sometimes.

Chimu Palace

Chan Chan, Chimu Empire

12th moon, day 5, near midnight

In the darkness, Shi's eyes were filled with images of her infant brother tucked beautifully in the grasp of her mother. The sound of gentle waves was replaced, at first, by his tender laugh that grew increasingly distorted as if by some evil force until it resembled a frantic scream.

This was not fear but torture.

In a frantic motion, Shi sat up, ending any hopes she had of sleep. Helpless; powerless; and governed by gods, kings, and fate, she sat alone and terrified. The king's furrowed, clay-red brows jutting from the wall piece seemed to mock her as she lay in bed. His half smile grew ever more ominous as the thought of morning loomed larger.

She grasped the llama wool tightly, feeling the individual fibers and the coarse bits of clay infused within. Her torn heart lashed out at the flattering depiction of the king. Every fiber within her wanted to jump out of her skin, rip up the textile she had spent all day creating, and tear down the walls around her.

Even the stars mocked her. They had been mocking her since birth, along with the rest of her kind, those born without status or privilege.

Disrupting the cool stillness of the night, she stood up and glared menacingly at the glorified image of the king, the symbol of her pain on the wall piece.

Shi—the 16-year-old daughter of a peasant fisherman—took a stand.

Returning frantically to the stockpile of materials, she grabbed a heap of llama wool and the clay-red dye and got to work creating the vision that she couldn't get out of her head.

Poised and with dignity for the first time since the sun last rose, Shi was resolute in her defiance. A burning intensity from within her very core seeped into her bloodstream and commandeered her entire being. She would be heard, if only just barely.

Chimu Palace

Chan Chan, Chimu Empire

12th moon, day 6, morning

As dawn broke, Shi looked up to the sun and then at the sea. The air seemed dry, perhaps even drier than yesterday, and belly-up fish, perhaps in greater numbers than yesterday, lined the beaches.

Regardless, destiny had spoken. The weather would be the weather, and the gods would be the gods.

Shi's exhausted hands used the last of their reserves to put the final touches on the wall piece. Upon finishing, her eyelids, as heavy as boulders, refused to reopen. The spirit that took hold of her wilted, and she passed out, exhausted from her labour.

As the first rays of light lanced above the walls of the tower, the king's servant reappeared only to find Shi collapsed in the centre of the room. She was curled up like an infant next to a wall piece the width of a small fishing boat and the height of a small child.

Searching for the king's familiar face, his rigid cheek bones and powerful eyes, she found 100 profiles of a small child in its place—10 rows of 10. The child looked not unlike Shi's 6-year-old brother.

The servant carefully eyed the finished wall piece. Inside the stark red lines, she saw a crisscrossed story of fishermen and their fish, of farmers and their crops, of servants, of weavers, of powerlessness.

Shi awoke to the servant standing before her, bewildered, shocked, thrilled, but mostly afraid, with a single tear rolling down her cheek.

In a half-woken stupor, Shi stroked the wall piece, wrapping herself in its majesty. She mused about its durability, its stability, and its genuineness that spoke to and for the people. She tenderly handed the 100 profiles to the awe-struck servant.

Perhaps out of sheer exhaustion, perhaps out of absolute distress, but more likely out of sadness, Shi began to feel light-headed again.

As her right hand released the wall piece, fuzziness began to cloud her vision. Her knees grew weak, and momentum slowly pushed her toward the ground.

Her narrowed vision caught only a glimpse of the wicked sun now just above the palace walls and the clay-red wool jawlines of her little brother.

In this moment, fear was relinquished, and out of the fuzziness emerged clarity.

Shi wondered if the king felt like a string sometimes.

She hoped so!

Discussion Questions

1) When a society is dependent on one source of food, such as fish from the sea or a single crop, what happens if all of a sudden that food source vanishes? Look up the word *monoculture* on the internet and then look up the Great Famine of Ireland. How is the situation described in Shi's village similar to the Great Famine?

2) Why are the bureaucrats in the seventh paragraph of part two planning buildings and canals? Do government bureaucrats plan the same type of things today?

3) Why does Shi ask if the gods require a sacrifice?

4) The main story in Homer's *The Odyssey* is about Odysseus's 18-year journey home from Troy. While he is away, his wife, Penelope, devises a way of keeping the suitors (men who would marry her and thus become king) at bay. She promises that she will choose one when she finishes the cloth she is weaving; to keep delaying the day when she will have to choose a new husband, each night Penelope sneaks into the room where the loom is and undoes that day's weaving. Compare how Penelope uses her weaving with how Shi uses hers.

5) Imagine that you are the king in the scene described at the end of section two. What do you think he is thinking? Do you think he is as powerful as he looks?

FATIMA

Zahida Rahemtulla

The following excerpts were found in the diary of Fatima Ibn Muhammad al-Ayyubi, who lived between the years of 1186 and 1221 in Nishapur, a city in the Khorasan province in what is now northeastern Iran. Although Fatima survived the earthquake that hit Nishapur in 1208, she died at the age of 35 following the 1220 Mongol invasions and massacre led by Genghis Khan, which wiped out nearly all of the city's population.

Esfand, the twelfth month, 1198, 12 years old

I learned to write under Baba's watchful gaze in the soft orange glow of an oil lamp. Together in the *andaruni,* Baba showed me how to make words live on paper. To this day my memories of Baba and our studies remain clear. I remember the thick carpets, the stillness of the enclosed workroom, and my grandfather's gentle voice intoning the alphabet, announcing each letter with a tap of his walking stick.

My back against the pillows of the workroom, perched on the floor of cushions, I would eagerly try to soak in the 32 letters of the alphabet, marvelling at how they could be reconfigured to make new words, formed on my grandfather's lips and given to my ears.

This was the alphabet that made the words of the Quran and my favourite verses of Omar Khayyam. It was my favourite part of the day when, after the sun had gone down and we had performed the dusk call to prayer, we would huddle back into the world of text.

I tried to hold back my excitement, for I knew it was not proper for a girl to be so eager, but Baba didn't seem to mind. When the time to study came, after he had rolled up his prayer mat for the evening, he would say, "Come, *Janoom,* let us continue with our letters." I would follow him into the andaruni workroom, and the evening would begin.

Baba was the only one who really had the time to teach me, since Mother didn't know how to read and Father was busy at the courts. Hassan and the others spent their free time accompanying Father to the courts to learn how to make the witness lists.

Father was very thorough in training Hassan, who would one day be *mozakk* himself. He didn't want to compromise his growing reputation. "Look how competent the son is," he hoped his superiors would say. "It is only because of the father's rigorous training."

At that time, Father hadn't started holding hadith classes. However, there were growing rumours that he would soon be asked by the *qadi* to do so, and father was doing everything to prove himself worthy of such an honour.

Hassan, Tariq, and Salim attended hadith classes at the madrasah. I would stay home and help Mother. They would come back with a vocabulary larger than the previous day, flaunting their ability to count and cite entire passages of the Quran from memory. But I didn't mind, because I had Baba's lessons.

Mother didn't object to Baba's teaching me so long as I had finished my chores, prepared the evening meal, and kept the water tank full with buckets from the well. Father had even heard of some girls in Nishapur who were formally taking such lessons and reasoned that at the very least it might make me more of an appealing match.

So there we were, Baba and I, his walking stick against the wall, him leaning over me making out letters in deep concentration. I would stick out my tongue as I dipped the quill into the inkpot before my next attempt. Baba had saved the paper from when he was still *mozakkī*. It was made by a Jewish paper-maker who used an old Chinese recipe to turn white mulberry branches into pulp.

Besides letters, Baba had many stories. In fact, he had such a repertoire that I used to think the only place he could possibly store them was in his beard. Each time he groomed it, I grew anxious that they would be lost. I wished I could grow a beard of my own so I could store them forever.

We would sit by the *khoursi*, and Baba's voice would illuminate the darkened room. After he told me a story, he would always say, "Goodnight, Janoom, may your dreams be as sweet as roses and as pure as the water in the finest of Nishapur's underground canals." And with that, he would unravel his turban, untie his bedroll, and give in to sleep.

Sometimes Baba told me stories he had heard in the marketplace, other times rumours about the royal court or the latest reported whisperings from the harem. Sometimes, if Baba wasn't too tired, he would recite the verses he could remember of the great Nishapuri poet Omar Khayyam. Baba was only about three years old when Omar Khayyam passed away, but his family had been well acquainted with the family of tent-makers from which Khayyam came.

Then one day Baba laid out his bedroll and never woke up. The next morning I went to his bedroll and tried to prod him, but Mother said quietly that he had gone on a journey to Allah.

They say that when someone goes on a journey or a long travel, if you steal something they own, you make sure that they will one day come back to you.

I have Baba's book.

Farvardin, the first month, 1201, 15 years old

Two Nowruz have come and gone since Baba passed away. This is the third. I kiss everyone in the family on the cheek early in the morning, and we celebrate with coffee and rosewater.

I remember how Baba used to love seeing the first green and the budding of the violet and white hyacinths that Nowruz brought us.

Mother and I set vases of roses and plates of almonds, fruit, and pastries throughout the house. As we do every year, we cooked the white fish and garnished it with coriander, parsley, and mint.

Even though much time has passed since Baba went away and I long ago stopped wearing my mourning clothes, I still miss him very much.

Whenever I start to feel the wetness in my eyes, I distract myself with this verse of Omar Khayyam. I don't know why, but it makes me feel better.

> And that inverted Bowl we call The Sky,
> Whereunder crawling coop't we live and die,
> Lift not thy hands to It for help—for It
> Rolls impotently on as Thou or I.

Ordibehesht, the second month, 1201, 15 years old

These days Mother and Father speak frequently about finding me a match, determined not to let another Nowruz pass with me still unmarried. It makes me nervous, and I am constantly fiddling with the fringe of my headscarf to soothe my anxiety, which drives Mother crazy.

Khordad, the third month, 1201, 15 years old

This afternoon, when Yasmin visited, Mother tried to broach the subject of my marriage with her to see if she could be of any help. However, as usual, Yasmin was preoccupied with her own troubles. For once, I welcomed her theatrical banter. I didn't even mind how loud she spoke so long as it kept Mother distracted from thinking about my marriage. I went inside to fetch them tea.

Though she had just come from next door, Yasmin was out of breath. She heaved herself into our courtyard, plopping her bottom onto one of the cushions on the floor, and immediately began complaining about her husband's temporary wife. "The evil eye of that woman," she said, grinding the few teeth she had left and wagging her finger. Yasmin was convinced that she had cast a spell on her youngest son, who was dying of consumption.

"And just imagine," she said, "if they have children together!" She worried about becoming the type of household where not only the wives but also the children of the different marriages were constantly arguing.

If Yasmin's children grew up to be anything like their mother, I could see how this would be a problem. It was not that Yasmin had a wicked spirit—in fact, her heart was quite big—but she had the curse of a bad temper.

Besides her own problems, Yasmin was deeply engrossed with the problems of others. This afternoon, she told Mother of a neighbour's neighbour who was suing her husband for divorce on the grounds of his impotence. "Poor man," she said, clicking her tongue in pity and sighing an exaggerated sigh. "At least he won't have to endure the burden of losing his dowry though."

What bothered Yasmin most about this was not the situation itself but the fact that she felt she could solve it but wouldn't be allowed to. "The answer," she said, "is of course dates."

More softly, with her mischievous, gap-toothed smile, and so only Mother and I could hear, she said, "The date left in milk causes powerful erections. If one drinks this milk regularly with cinnamon, genital properties will be irrepressible."

Yasmin knew a lot about these things, because she was selling herbal remedies in order to collect money for her daughter's future dowry. "You can never start too early," she would lecture. But she couldn't suggest her remedy to the couple, because it would be rude, and everyone was already mad at Yasmin for knowing everyone else's business all the time anyway.

Then we heard about the woman who was still haggling with a husband who had divorced her and remarried but still hadn't returned the dowry. The poor thing hadn't managed to get pregnant despite having taken every imaginable herb and having visited every possible healer.

By the time Yasmin left with the woes of the neighborhood on her shoulders, dusk had fallen, and I went inside with mother to sit near the khoursi.

It was colder, and mother and I were silent. I wrapped the lambskin blanket tighter around us and looked into Mother's eyes for warmth, but they were far away, somewhere in the future, worrying about my wedding.

Mehr, the seventh month, 1201, 15 years old

The sky has been read by Nishapur's finest astrologer, and the message from the stars dictates that I am to be married in three months. A match has been found. He is the nephew of the qadi, son of a prominent dignitary, and Mother and Father are very pleased with having secured the tie.

His name is Sameer.

The marriage will take place in our house, and for weeks Mother has been arranging and rearranging every single item in the house—including, Father jokes, every piece of dust. I must start creating the gifts for my dowry.

Mother and I prepare the tokens I will give to him. We embroider endlessly, but I still manage to steal time to write.

Both Mother and Father agree that there will be no stinginess when it comes to the wedding. They want to impress my future husband's family. So they make sure we have an attorney conducting the agreement instead of a cleric, and they insist on at least eight days of wedding celebrations.

Mother declares only the finest harvest of nuts, raisins, and pomegranates will be laid out for consumption. We will restock the storage shafts that hold the oil, vinegar, honey, barley, sheep fat, and dried fruit before the wedding. Everything must be brand new.

Dey, the 10th month, 1201, 15 years old

This morning I carefully put on my thick velvet robe with its intricate pattern of roses, and underneath, silk trousers saved especially for the occasion. I have put kohl on my eyes and incense on my clothes. It is the day of the ceremony.

After Father and my brothers receive the groom, I arrive through a half-open door with Mother and her sisters.

The room has been laid out with our finest carpets and pottery. Mother even borrowed some pieces from Yasmin to decorate. The khoursi is draped with our most expensive blankets.

I stand in front of Sameer but stare at the floor in order to put off meeting his eyes. I see a speck of dust and Father's hairy toes.

Raising my head, I catch sight of his turban, all the while still avoiding his eyes. It could only have been made from the finest silk. I think of all of the taverns and traders' hands it must have passed through to have landed there on his head in front of me. Suddenly distracted, I want to touch it. How it must feel! I imagine the tightest knots and the brightest dyes.

Our respective parties state the terms of the marriage settlement and ask Sameer and I for individual consent. Then, finally, the attorney confirms the agreement and authenticates the marriage document with his seal.

Eight days later

It is almost time to leave now. In accordance with the financial terms Sameer's family agreed to, money, rings, and presents of clothes and jewels are bundled and dispatched with my trousseau.

I offer my husband the tokens we created with my dowry. In broad daylight, the camels are loaded, ready for departure to my new home.

It is a huge load, and judging by the silk of Sameer's turban, I don't think many of the items were borrowed to impress us. Wives often complain they are taken away and given back to their rightful owners after the wedding. Some brides even find out upon arriving that the boxes were empty, added only to make the groom's family seem generous. I see Mother discreetly check if one of the boxes that looked rather light was empty. It isn't.

That same night, I am transported to my husband's house in a litter, carried by the same camels that carried my trousseau and gifts from Sameer's family during the day. From head to toe I am covered, and over my first veil is draped another veil of silk reaching my waist so that no one can glimpse my figure. No one wants spells of the envious cast following their wedding.

My camel has sand-coloured hair and kohl on its eyes for protection from the sun. Our eyes match. The camel's nose is decorated with turquoise tassels and pink woven cloth. But it is ill tempered. I wonder if it will turn back and take me home.

On the way to Sameer's home, we pass the covered bazaar and spice market with its burlap bags overflowing with dried lemon, turmeric, and saffron. We pass the saddle makers, slipper makers, and liver-kebab sellers and the boys who shout, "Coffee! Coffee!" but end up being drowned out by the noise of the bazaar.

We pass the *hammam* where Mother and I bathe. We pass the inn where weary caravans and travellers rest, and we pass several irritated mule drivers causing traffic havoc. We pass the meat market and the bazaar where metal beaters pound teacups and spoons out of tin. We pass the mosque.

Even though I am not leaving Nishapur, I feel the need to say goodbye to all these places.

When I start to feel the wetness in my eyes, I distract myself with this verse of Omar Khayyam's.

> And that inverted Bowl we call The Sky,
> Whereunder crawling coop't we live and die,
> Lift not thy hands to It for help—for It
> Rolls impotently on as Thou or I.

I don't know why, but it makes me feel better. The camel moves forward.

Discussion Questions

1) Fatima admires the letters that make up Arabic writing. Look up the Quran and *The Rubaiyat of Omar Khayyam* and see if you can find what meant so much to her.

2) Fatima's brothers are all studying at a school. Why isn't she?

3) Why is it so important to Fatima's parents that they find a husband for her? Why isn't she able to choose her husband for herself?

4) Yasmin tells Fatima how to deal with what today we would call erectile dysfunction. Why is it that women are usually the ones who have knowledge of herbs and potions?

5) At the wedding, Fatima is struck by the quality of the silk in Sameer's turban. Look up the Silk Road and figure out how long it would have taken the silk to arrive in Fatima's village.

HOSKI

Alisha Sunderji

Grandma's face is weathered and creased like the red earth when it has not rained for many weeks. Her voice is rich but quiet, and when she speaks it's almost as though she's whispering. She weighs every word; everything about her is calm and deliberate. Grandma, my shinali, often watches me weave, sometimes telling me stories of our people, the Diné. My favourite is the story of how the Diné learned to weave.

The holy ones advised Spider Woman that she could weave a map of the universe and the patterns of the spirit beings in the night sky. At first she did not know what they meant, but she was curious. One day, as she was exploring the land and gathering food, she came across a young tree. She touched it and wrapped her fingers around one of the branches. When she released her hand, she realized that a string that was streaming from the middle of her palm was attached to the branch. Soon she started manipulating the string, wrapping it around different branches. Spider Woman quickly realized she was creating a pattern and, at that very moment, knew this was the weaving the holy people had told her about.

Spider Woman returned home and showed her new skill to her husband, Spider Man. The holy ones heard of her learning and instructed Spider Man to build a weaving loom and the necessary tools needed to weave. Spider Woman began to sing the weaving song given to her by the holy ones as she wove on her loom.

Grandma tells me that songs make clothes strong. She also has told me that the two main beams of the loom represent pillars holding up the sky and keeping Mother Earth secure. The third beam at the foot of the two pillars is the earth on which we live. The fourth beam, placed at the top, represents the sunbeams and rainbows that protect Mother Earth.

I feel a light tapping on my shoulder, pulling me away from Spider Woman's story. Grandma is standing beside me, pointing to the tangled mess of string in the middle of my loom. "Hoski," she says, "pay attention. Remember, to weave, placing layers upon layers of wool, is to create life. Weaving teaches us to learn from our mistakes, but you should try to avoid making them altogether." Grandma's tone is stern, but her expression is kind. When I was younger, she used to tell me and my big sister Doli that Talking God would speak through the wind and tell Spider Woman where to find disobedient children. Once she found them, she would boil them and then eat them. The white streaks at the top of Spider Rock, the mountain near our home, says Grandma, are where the bones of bad children remain, bleaching the rocks to this day.

Mother's voice rings out through my sleep. "Hoski," she says, "we are low on wood. Get up." Collecting wood is my job, so I reluctantly peel off the warm blankets and run out of our hogan. It is just before dawn, the moon is still hanging in the sky, the air is cold. I am wrapped in my blanket, but the cold wind stings my cheeks. I see the dwindling pile of kindling. I am an expert wood gatherer; without thinking, my feet lead me to a dry log I recently discovered.

A cool breeze tickles my neck and rattles the leaves of the sagebrush. All is quiet except for the sound of the dry earth crunching beneath my feet. I can see the outline of our hogan in the distance. By the time I return home, the sky is pink and bright. It is time to build a fire and start preparing for the day. Collecting firewood is not so bad. The worst is when Grandma's harsh words rouse me from sleep. "Get up and run, Hoski. There is work to be done. If you sleep you will be weak—what good will sleep bring you?" she often tells me. Those mornings are hard. Sometimes I leave the hogan in tears, but I keep running despite the cold winds blowing against my tired body.

Once I remember Grandma seeing my tear-stained face after a morning run. She pulled me aside and whispered in my ear, "Hoski, look around you." My mother was preparing food in the hogan, while Doli was washing our clothes. "Do you see that they are all working hard?" she asked. "I've had to work hard my whole life—as a young girl like you, as a mother, and now as a grandmother. You must become strong, Hoski." She told me the story of when the Navajo woke to the first dawning and realized that life was to be a continuous struggle for survival.

They knew that throughout their lives they would have to face the four monsters: old age, poverty, sickness, and death. These monsters were left by the killers of all evils, the Twin War Gods, in the beginning of our world, to challenge the Navajo and create obstacles that help us become stronger. Grandma smiled with pride when she told me this story and said, "The harshness of the bitter wind will give you strength Hoski."

Today there is a buzz of excitement in the air. It is the last day of Doli's kinaalda ceremony. The ceremony celebrates her entry to womanhood, and our whole family has gathered to wish her good luck. For the past three days, Doli has slipped out of the hogan early in the morning to run east toward the sun, stirring up a billowing cloud of dust at her feet. "Doli," says Grandma, "you are running toward your new life. Remember to take this strength and these good thoughts with you into the world."

Last night, while everyone was sleeping, I crept over to Doli's bed. The moonlight that trickled in from the smoke hole of our hogan lit only half her face. She smiled peacefully as she slept. I thought of all that had happened in the past few days. It all started when she came running to me, her eyes wide in panic, pointing to the dark stains of blood on her blanket. We ran together to Grandma, whose eyes twinkled as she listened to Doli's story. She smiled and said, "Doli, you are becoming a woman."

Since the beginning of the ceremony, Doli has been working hard. Strands of her long black hair clung to her sweaty face as she ground mounds and mounds of cornmeal all day long. While she did this, friends and family members came by, ordering her to cut wood or other tasks. She faced a torrent of orders and demands, all the while rhythmically grinding the meal. I asked Doli afterwards why everyone was being so demanding. She smiled knowingly. "They don't want me to be lazy, Hoski, that's all. We have to work hard our whole lives; that's all they mean to say. Don't look so frightened."

The quiet calm of her breathing and the silence of the night soothed me. I felt as though things would be different after tomorrow, as though Doli would be farther away from me than she is now. Sadness grew inside of me but also joy, as the kinaalda is a happy event in a woman's life. I lay down beside her and wrapped myself in her blankets until sleep gently washed over me.

I woke up when Doli was leaving the hogan for her final run toward the rising sun. She gave me a quick smile before skirting out the blanket door. Our hogan is cozy and warm. Sometimes when I can't sleep, I like to count the cedar logs that make up the walls and roof. The curved walls meet at the smoke hole, a small circular opening at the very top of the roof. The smoke hole is for more than just letting smoke escape from the fire. It is so that evil spirits will get blown away when the medicine man sings his ghost-chasing chant.

The outside is covered by packed, dried mud. I remember when we built our home, how family and friends helped us for an entire day. We had to finish before it got dark; otherwise evil ones would come and cause sickness. When it was finished, a medicine man came to bless our home, asking for happiness from all directions, from the earth and the sky, with the promise of shelter to anyone in need. The hogan is a sacred dwelling for the Diné. It is built in harmony so that our family can be together to endure life's hardships and become a part of the harmony that exists between the sacred mountains, Mother Earth, and Father Sky.

After gathering more wood, I come back to witness the final part of the ceremony. The air is sweet and warm. The cornmeal that Doli worked so hard to grind has filled a deep pit outside our hogan. Baked by the sun, the huge cake will feed everyone. A small crowd has formed. At the centre is Doli, on her stomach, lying on a blanket. Mother is kneeling over her, pressing on different parts of her body. She is moulding Doli; the rub will give Doli energy and help her grow.

Friends and family are chatting loudly and singing—everyone is excited for her. Once mother has done her moulding, Doli stands up and walks around the crowd, lifting small children up to her shoulders in the hopes that she will help them grow tall and strong. She touches the elderly, including Grandma, as it is believed that during this time Doli is a magical being and has the power to heal. A piece of corn cake is passed to me; it sticks to my fingers. I eat it in small pieces, savouring each bite.

I hear the sound of beating drums and shaking rattles before I see the bright orange flames of the bonfire. Above, the dark winter sky is punctuated by bright stars. I can see the smoky whiteness of my breath. A crowd has formed a ring around the fire. Anaba is sitting in front of her family's hogan, wrapped tightly in blankets. Dancing flames are reflected in her dark, empty eyes.

Anaba has been ill for a while now. Grandma tells me that sickness is caused when there is a lack of balance in a person's life. The Diné believe in hózhó, or "walking in beauty," the idea that all things in life are connected. All things possess a spirit and power and can influence each other. To walk in beauty means to be in touch with all parts of the world, to see one's mind, body, and spirit as connected to other people, communities, and the world as a whole.

Something in Anaba's life fell out of balance, and she lost her way on the path of beauty. Perhaps she touched an object struck by lightning or came across a snake. Her family consulted a hataalii, or medicine man, to identify her illness and recommend the appropriate healing ceremony. And so for nine days, Anaba's family, friends, and community would gather to perform the yeibeichei, or night chant ceremony, to restore her health.

During this period, the hataalii invites Talking God, the leader of other gods, to cure Anaba's illness. Looking around the blazing fire, I realize that all the people who have gathered here tonight want to help Anaba and in turn benefit from the ceremony's collective healing power.

Suddenly, the sound of beating drums becomes louder. Out of the darkness emerge three figures, each wearing a mask. Their bodies are painted with white ash, and they are only wearing small skirts of wool despite the cold weather. The features of their grotesque masks are half lit by the fire light. Grandma whispers in my ear, "Hoski, do you see the man with the eagle feathers? He represents Talking God. And the one who looks like a clown is Water Sprinkler." The last figure I recognize. He is Yasskidi, the hunchback. They stomp their feet in unison, shaking their rattles, moving slyly around the fire.

The drums get louder and louder. My heart is pounding. The sound of the drums vibrates through my entire body. The dancers are moving faster and faster. The repetitive chants, the rattles, and the sound of beating drums are hypnotic. I find myself chanting songs without thinking. My skin tingles. Here I feel the strength and beauty of my community. Here I belong.

My blanket is almost complete. Even though Grandma's eyes are weak, she feels across the surface of the fabric, gently tracing its bumps and ridges. "Hoski," she says with a smile in her voice, "your weaving is getting better." She adds mysteriously, "Hoski, I have someplace to show you. Come with me." Grandma's face reveals nothing. I follow her outside the hogan, past the garden and the small brook. We walk in silence, listening only to the gentle sound of dry earth cracking beneath our feet. After walking for a while, Grandma points to a patch of ground right in front of her feet. There is a lone tree a few feet away.

"Hoski, I remember vividly the day you were born. You cried and cried once you left your mother's body. And your big eyes! Once you stopped crying, your eyes searched us hungrily—like they were starving for colour and for our faces." She chuckles quietly to herself. I have heard this story many times, but each time it always sounds different. She taps the earth with her foot. "Here, Hoski, is where your cord is buried. This place is important. It marks where your life changed from being nourished by your mother to being nurtured by Mother Earth, your spiritual mother. You, like all the Diné, share a sacred bond with Mother Earth. Remember this."

I wonder why Grandma has chosen this moment to share this story with me. The more I learn about the Diné, the more I realize that my identity is tied to this place, the earth and its people. I slip my hand into my grandmother's. She smiles, and together we begin to walk back home.

Discussion Questions

1) Why does Hoski's grandmother say that songs make the clothes strong? In reality, what is it about weaving that makes the cloth strong? Look up the terms *warp* and *woof* and see how they define some of what Hoski's grandmother is telling her about weaving and cloth.

2) Hoski is probably overstating things in the beginning of the second section when she says her feet lead her to a log "without thinking." Yet why is it important that she remember where she found logs?

3) The Navajo's tales were formed long before they had any contact with Christian civilization. It is interesting, however, that the Navajo believed in the four monsters old age, poverty, sickness, and death, while Christians believe in the Four Horseman of the Apocalypse as described in the Book of Revelations. Look up the Four Horseman of the Apocalypse and compare what each horseman represents with the four Navajo monsters.

4) What is the purpose of the ceremony that follows after Doli has her first period?

5) Hoski tells us that Anaba becomes ill because Anaba's life has "fallen out of balance." Today, we know that Anaba likely became ill because of bacteria, a virus, or a disease such as cancer. At about the time this story takes place, however, Europeans still believed that disease was caused by an imbalance in the four humors: black bile, yellow bile, phlegm, and blood. Look up these terms and see what a European doctor in Anaba's time period would have said was the cause of her illness.

Adjoa

Lara Berliner

As she walks out onto the streets of Kumasi amid the cries of food and cloth vendors and the sounds of yet another one of those large ships back from the New World, Adjoa thinks only of the upcoming evening Nnwankoro. This time her song must be special. This time she must show all those other women that even though misfortune has befallen her family, she will not be afraid. But what story to tell? What message should she pass on to the community and to her son before he is swept away by the ocean on a tall ship destined for an unknown land and a life of harsh labour?

A mother's job is never easy, she thinks to herself, for with the blessing of nine children comes also the curse of caring deeply for them all. She hurries along toward her husband's market stall; there is no more time for such thoughts. It is not far now. The sun is high in the sky, and he will be expecting her shortly.

She said she would watch the booth. The city looks lovely bathed in the sunlight. Although she hates the ships that come into the port to collect the riches of her land—to cart them away in their deep bellies, to sell the goods somewhere far away—she must admit, if only to herself, that the ships are quite magical. The sails are as white as the ivory they carry, the masts carved and painted with African gold, and the decks constantly scrubbed by slaves. She shudders at the thought of her son Nùm aboard those floating monsters.

A few moons ago, or perhaps a little longer, and Nùm's fate would not have been so severe. Adjoa could have perhaps lived up to the expectations of her name, which means "peace," and could have arranged for him to work for a wealthy family in the city or maybe even as a slave in the emperor's palace hauling water for the imperial baths. There he would have been legally protected. At least Adjoa could have rested peacefully knowing that her son would not be harmed because of the just laws of the emperor king. Surely he is just. He is the one who implements the law. And he will be kind to her husband today. Surely he will be. He is supposed to be a good king and a kind man. He will cancel the debts.

Slavery within Africa is decreasing. However, due to the growing opportunity for riches in the export of its young men and women to foreign lands, simple commodities to be bought and sold, there has been a significant rise in the number of those ships in the port and the number of foreigners who walk her streets and barter with the vendors.

She sighs as she thinks of her child's misfortune. Nùm is the fifth child, a most unlucky number, so his fate does not come to her as an absolute surprise. Still, her husband's debts have brought a great tragedy to the family. Her husband. Yes, of course. She realizes she must really hurry now. He will be expecting her.

She scurries past the fresh fruit stalls and finally turns into the familiar lane of the market. Her husband is sitting in front of the rows of cocoa beans and other nuts, perched on a small stool like a bird. His dark eyes are kind and similar to her first son's. *"Kobena, maakyØé.* Good morning, my husband," Adjoa greets this man with whom she has lived and shared her life for the past 20 years.

She has known him since she was a young girl training to be a cloth maker and had to run through the market streets every morning before dawn to arrive at her training with the elder women. What was it that happened that one fateful day during the dry season—or was it the rains? Was that it? She suddenly, in all of her clumsiness, tripped over her own two feet and fell straight into the arms of a young man. He must have been setting out his food for the day, fresh with the smell of nuts and spices and cacao. He said, "Be careful there, or you might send my wares rolling all the way to our Denkyira neighbours. I am sure they would not mind, but I, on the other hand . . ." Was that what he said? Was that how he said it? She could no longer remember.

Leaving her dream, she realizes that her husband is ready to leave, waiting to say goodbye, expecting her to wish him luck in his meeting. "Today is the day, my Adjoa. Today is the day that everything will fall into place and happen as it should. The caring and gracious and powerful"—he takes long pauses between words, she notices—"and great Emperor Osei Tutu is going to see me, is going to receive me as a visitor in his palace. I am one of many who have made pilgrimages to see him this special day, but he is going to watch over me as I bow and pledge my loyalty to his empire. And then, my darling Adjoa, he will fix our problems.

With one magical swoop of his wand, our debts will be paid. After today, not even Kwaku Ananse, that tricky spider, that mystic being of our ancestors, will be able to shred our happiness."

His voice rises, full of hope, as he reaches the dramatic end of his speech. She half smiles but does not raise her eyes from the ground, does not want to curse the luck her family needs. "Shh, do not call on such tricky beings. Go now, quickly! The gods of our ancestors and Nyame, our God, and Asaase Afua, the mother goddess, are all smiling on you. I can feel it!" She squeezes his hand once, unable to meet his gaze, and ushers him off into the noise of the market. Then silence. A sudden rush of peace enters her mind and clears it so she is again able to think.

As Adjoa takes her place on the stool in front of the stall, she thinks of the emperor, the mighty unifier of the Ashanti Empire, sitting on his golden stool, the seat of power and decision making for all the land—perhaps even the land of the Denkyira neighbours as well. It must be a large weight on his shoulders to have the future of so many people in his hands.

Her twin girls will one day be potential marriage matches for the king's son. Many moons will pass before they will be ready though, and until that moment she must bear this weight, for childhood is no time for fears. It is instead a time for happiness, as the elders rightly believe, and did she not know immense happiness when she was young? Of course she did. She knew all of life's simple joys.

Life became harder once she married. Life becomes harder for everyone after marriage—suddenly there are mouths to feed and others to take care of, others that you would give all of yourself for. She used to love to dance, to perform in the community rituals and gatherings, to dance around the fires and feel the beat of the drums pulsing through her body. Dum-de-dum dum,

dum-de-dum dum—oh, was that it? Or was it dum dum de-dum dum de, dum dum de-dum dum de?

She taps her feet along to the invisible drums and the rhythm inside her head. Dum-de-dum-de-da. No, she decides, she must try to shield her children from some of life's harsh realities until it is necessary to face them, until they are prepared. She must try her best for all of them, even her fifth son, the unlucky one. Their souls are pure. Besides, she thinks to herself, the twins are not even of the age of the puberty rite. No need to beat the traditional iron hoe until the moment when it is necessary to announce to the world, to the community—to the elder women, really—that her girls have reached the age and life stage where she will no longer be able to protect them. At that point, the cold winds of life will be let in no matter how she tries to be bigger than the gusts and block the wind's every entrance. Her girls—all of them, not only the twins—will know in time what it is to be forbidden to cook for the men or to enter the religious house during their time of the month, what it is to live like an outcast for a week at a time.

You should also be thankful, Adjoa, she scolds herself. *You have had much success in life,* she reminds herself. What of the power the twins give her over other, less fertile women of the community, less capable of bearing so many and such healthy children? What of the social status, the pride, and the luck they bring? And the honour they will bestow on the family when they marry into the royal family. Perhaps she should mention all of that in her song tonight. Oh yes, the gathering tonight. She almost forgot. *Yes, Adjoa, focus on the good in your life. The sorrows will surely still be there to think about in the morning, after your husband's return.*

What was it her husband mentioned? Kwaku Ananse? Oh how that reminds her of simpler days, of childhood. After all, childhood was not that long ago, even though the years, however few, have changed her so as to make her unrecognizable. How she used to love the myths, the stories her grandfather would tell her of distant places and foreign people, the traveller's tales he would recount, the spider stories that captivated her young self with the adventures and mischief of Kwaku Ananse. She used to love the stories and all the interesting ideas they put into her head.

There was always so much to think about after her grandfather finished that she often could not fall asleep for hours. She would toss and turn, turning the stories over and over in her mind. She imagined she was the beautiful princess, or the caravan leader, or the trickster spirit. Those were more carefree days—her destiny was to become a weaver, a very respectable occupation for a woman, and training was her only responsibility. It would have been a profitable business too because of all the trade in cloth.

Those Portuguese did not realize what they started. Click, click, click. *Wait!* she calls to the rhythm in her head, but she is too late. It is lost to the sounds of a European official walking by. The white men who come on those white ships do not often walk by her market stall. The hired administrators, as they are called, rule the streets from high above and hardly dare to step from their special buildings into the noise and chaos of the world around them. They answer to the king. And currently the king is stronger than ever because of the many tribes brought into the Ashanti Empire. *But still, that man's clicking heels have no place in my market place, just as those men do not have as large a place in society as they would like to believe. And it should stay that way. They are foreign and do not belong!* The words echo defiantly in her mind. They do not belong. She chuckles to herself at her mischievous thoughts as the man click clacks on by the stall.

Empire! She still cannot comprehend the meaning of that word. A strong and powerful land, a unified force of the people which, she supposes, are meant to work toward a common good. Or is it merely a title given to those who are successful warriors and who can conquer many kingdoms? The empire is recent enough news that she will sing about it tonight and about the generosity of the king who welcomed visitors from the empire at large to his place this day in order that he might hear the needs of the public and rule a contented empire.

Did he really state that today was a day to waive people's debts? She cannot remember anymore what is real and what is fiction and what are thoughts she has made up in her head in order that she might hope them to be the truth. *No more doubts until my husband returns, for only then will I know what the truth is today.*

She begins to hum to herself and to collect her thoughts into an imaginary bundle of white linen cloth like the materials attached to the ships. She shields her eyes momentarily from the few specks of dust and sand and pebbles swirling around her feet that manage to reach her eyes. The times are changing as quickly as the wind, she realizes. The ships that are currently docked will soon be gone only to be replaced by others returning greedily for more.

Oh! How could I not see it before? I am fearful of change, she admits to herself. *And there are too many at once. I cannot be brave and face them head on. I am scared. And I am at the mercy of the winds and tides of change,* she hums to herself, *the tides of change.*

Later that evening she clears her throat, and in a deep, strong voice, she begins:

Time is a fickle thing.

Never does it halt when we ask it to,

Nor does it run faster as we wish,

And so time will pass as it must

And bring with it many changes.

I, for one, will soon embrace my son, perhaps for the last time,

And send him on his way

On a foreign ship,

Never to know of his journeys, successes, or even his tasks,

And most definitely, and most heartbreakingly,

Most probably never to know of his return.

But we, as one, as a people,

Must also face the coming days, the coming changes,

For we have no choice.

Our journeys as an empire will test our strength,

Our commitment, our perseverance. These will measure our strength.

Our emperor, atop his golden peak, is just and strong.

Let us continue to strengthen him.

Let us draw strength from our children, for their purity will shield us.

And guide us. And allow us to return from our journeys

Knowing the truth of our future.

Discussion Questions

1) This story is about the African slave trade. Look up the terms "triangle trade" and "middle passage." What do you think Adjoa knew of them?

2) In Canada today, women have fewer than two children. Adjoa had nine. Why would she consider this a blessing?

3) The great Emperor Osei Tutu is very powerful. But is he as powerful as the white men who command the sailing ships in the harbour?

4) Why is it said that "Life becomes hard for everyone after marriage"? Do we feel this way about marriage today?

5) Adjoa learns the word *empire* from the Portuguese men and has trouble understanding it. What is an empire? How large was the Portuguese Empire? Compare its size at its height to the size of the Roman Empire and the British Empire.

ANNE DE FERMONT

Nicolas Greenfield

Standing before the heavy wooden door, she breathed a sigh of relief. She had travelled far in the cold rain to arrive at her destination. The uncomfortable night spent on the ship from the port of Ville-Marie had left her with aching muscles and bones. Despite the pain, she felt numb.

It was mid-morning, and everyone seemed to have been forced inside the thick stone walls by the grim April weather. But not all! Those milking the cows had to brave the weather. It made the courtyard silent, almost mournful. God willing, she would be granted permission to live in the convent with the nuns. She wanted to dedicate herself to the Lord's work, to holy charity and worship.

She smiled as she forced herself to regain her composure. It would not do to look too excited. Looking about at the grey cobblestone courtyard, she paused a moment to smooth down her dress before knocking on the door. Following several moments of silence, she heard footsteps coming from within the wooden gateway. This was followed by the soft but audible click of the handle. Even before the door was fully open, Anne could see a short, portly sister.

The nun was clothed from head to foot in the habit and scapular of her order, leaving only her face visible. Noting the rain-soaked woman standing before her, the sister made no effort to hide her alarm and bewilderment. She was amazed that anyone, let alone an unescorted woman, would dare to brave this weather and blessed herself.

"My dear woman! Please, please step inside. You'll catch a cold standing out in that dreadful rain," said the nun, ushering the wet and shivering guest into the convent's entrance hall. Gathering a heavy wooden blanket from a nearby armoire, she added, "Put this on—it'll warm you up," as she pulled it around the woman's shoulders.

"Please, I assure you I am quite all right," the woman replied, smiling kindly before adding, "My name is Anne de Fermont. I travelled here along the St. Lawrence River from Ville-Marie."

"Travelling here? From Ville-Marie? Am I to assume you travelled all the way on your own? If so, it must be important."

"It is. Though only for me. I come with hope of not returning to the little I left behind. I—I want," she said, pulling her hand to her throat. "I mean, if you could allow me, I want to join your congregation, if such a thing is possible for a woman such as me."

"What do you mean, a woman such as you?" inquired the nun.

"I am not like you or the other sisters. I have been married—happily. My husband passed not two months ago. I am a widow."

The nun's demeanour softened at hearing those words. "I understand, but I can assure you that you are not the first widow to seek refuge in the grace of our Lord. But none of this is for me to decide. Come, there is a fire in the hearth in the anteroom on your right. Wait there, Madame de Fermont, and I will go and find our mother superior, with whom you must speak."

Anne seated herself on one of the pillowed chairs closest to the flame. Staring into the fire, she watched the dancing shapes move across the blaze, enhanced by the contrast between the bright flashing sparks and the billowing smoke that funnelled upward into the chimney. Yes, she had loved him. Her husband of almost a decade had been good to her, despite her repeated failures at providing him a child.

Her mother had been one of the *filles du roi* sent to New France by the king to help populate the New World by providing young, marriageable women. She recalled fondly the many evenings she had spent as a child learning womanly tasks, such as cooking, weaving, and the general arts of the housekeeper, from her mother, all the while listening to her stories of life in Paris. Her mother, having learned from a sister upon her arrival in Ville-Marie, also taught Anne to read as well as the foundation of the religion that she hoped was to become the focus of her daily life from now on.

She had been barely 12 years old when her father introduced her to Rénald de Fermont, an ex-military officer who had been awarded a small parcel of land by Seigneur Charles le Moyne de

Longueuil, across the river from Ville-Marie. Ever since their marriage shortly afterwards, Anne had devoted her life to taking care of her husband and his affairs. The two of them had made a happy home, despite the miscarriages. Rénald had been good to her. He had always treated her kindly and often had returned from his trips to different parts of New France with gifts for his young wife.

On one occasion, returning from a trip to Quebec, Rénald had given her a beautiful light blue gown that had come from Paris by way of a naval merchant. Anne had kept the gown hidden, wearing it only several months later at the village gathering celebrating the *Nouvel An*. They had danced late into the night, she and Rénald.

She heard two sets of footsteps, and before the mother superior entered the room, Anne banished the thoughts of past memories; reality came rushing back. Moments later, a tall woman stood before her in the doorway. Although her outfit was similar to that of the nun that had greeted Anne, no one could ever have confused the two.

The woman before Anne wielded an air of authority like none she had ever seen before. Her bearing, stern and powerful, seemed to enhance her size in the door frame, flooding the room with her authoritative presence. Her eyes burned with religious fervor yet were tinged with the deep shadow of one who has seen much grief and sorrow. A soft, motherly smile crept its way onto her lips, revealing the profound charity hidden beneath her stoic exterior.

"Hello, my child. You must be Anne de Fermont. I am Catherine de Montaigne, mother superior of the convent here in Quebec. Sister Dominique informed me of your arrival. Had we been told of your coming, we would have made arrangements to meet you. Tell me, are you well?"

"I am, Mother. I am deeply sorry if I have given you any cause for worry. This was not my intention. If I had had the time or the means, to announce my coming I would have done so. Sadly, I had already forsaken most of my earthly belongings prior to my departure. You see, I hope not to have need of them ever again."

"Yes, so Sister Dominique has informed me. It seems you have decided to come and join our sisterhood in your . . ." She paused briefly.

"Widowhood, Mother. My husband of a decade, Rénald de Fermont, may he rest in peace, is dead. He is now graced in the presence of our Lord."

"And for that I am well and truly sorry for you—to have born the pain of loss so early in your life. Many in your situation have come before, though none were so young as you. Surely you must still have young children to rear, if not land to till? Would you not rather see to their education before submitting yourself to the confines of the sisterhood?"

"I thank you for the sentiment. But no, Mother, I do not have children, and I suppose that is the reason why I have come. I am a barren widow who is not likely to remarry, and as my husband's lands legally came to me upon his death due to our custom, I would have had no one to pass them on to."

"So you conceded them?"

"Yes, Mother, to one of the neighbouring landowners. I see it as my first act of genuine charity."

"I understand," said Mother Superior, offering her tea. "And what of your life? Have you thought of all that will be left behind? Your daily occupations would find themselves quite changed were you to join our sisterhood."

"I have, Mother, but it is of no concern to me. I have lived the last years of my life as most young brides do when married to a landowner. Like my mother before me, I ran the household, though I suspect it was much easier work in the absence of children. I spent a great deal of time cooking, cleaning, sewing, and caring for my husband. When the housework was done, like so many others, I would go out into the fields and aid my husband in his daily work.

"He and I were close and shared much. With his teaching I learned to work the plow, to plant in the spring and harvest in the autumn. In the summer months, when Rénald would travel to the markets in Ville-Marie and beyond, I would stay behind and mind the farm on my own, taking full charge of the daily running of the land."

Waiting for a response from de Montaigne, Anne's gaze swept once more around the room before settling on a painting of the Madonna resting above the fireplace. The half-melted candles by the image indicated that the hearth below was not the only source of light in the wide stone room.

"These are tremendous physical feats for a woman, Anne de Fermont," replied Catherine de Montaigne. "In your voice I sense a great love for your husband and the land. Within these stone walls it is easy for me to forget the well-known strength of body and character of the women of our *Nouvelle France*. You must, however, be aware that much of the work to which we dedicate our lives here is of the mind and the heart."

"And I care for them as well. As my mother taught me numbers, I have long kept the books of my husband. He, bless his soul, was never one for working with numbers. As for the heart, I have already mentioned the donation of my belongings, and you see before you the result of the humility of my travelling," she added, indicating her drenched clothing. "As well, is it not a holy thing to care for one's husband in sickness as in health? Often I performed my wifely duties as my husband lay sick in bed, providing for him in all things, food or otherwise.

"My wedding vows, though I said them when I was still too young to fully understand their meaning, have always guided my actions. As I cared for my husband, I hope henceforth to care for my sisters. I want to give my aid freely in holy charity to the poor and the sickly in the hospitals of Quebec when it is needed. I want to help them and heal them. When all else fails, I want to be there to comfort them and aid them in their passing as I did with my husband."

This was the first time that Anne had ever spoken aloud of these things. The words, though difficult in their saying at the beginning, slowly began to flow out more smoothly and eloquently. More and more, the woman speaking to Catherine de Montaigne grew convinced of the truth behind her hopes. In speaking them, her plans became purpose.

In contrast, the mother superior, now seated, listened intently to Anne. She had not often seen such a mixture of hope and despair in a woman not three decades old. Catherine de Montagne believed that were Anne to join the Ursulines, she would do well within the sisterhood. She smiled again, this time making no effort to hide the joy she felt in her newfound discovery.

"Clearly your time travelling was not spent in idle waiting. I hope I did not offend you with my questions. Far be it from me to try to scare away one who desires to join our congregation. I simply wished to understand your thoughts and motivations, in fear that you may not have given proper contemplation to the weight of your intentions."

At this, Anne relaxed once more.

"I see now that I have no cause whatsoever for worry. If this is what you truly wish to do, then I will aid you in your designs. One does not, however, become a full sister overnight. You must first join the novitiate before completing your studies, after which you will be eligible for sisterhood."

Anne nodded, suddenly feeling small again before the mother superior seated across from her.

"If it pleases you, I will personally support you in your decision. We will see to your further education as well as to your housing, food, and clothing." Catherine de Montaigne stood and turned around, walking back toward the doorway.

Below the arch, she looked at Anne one more time and added, "I am truly glad you have come to us, Anne de Fermont. I will send Sister Dominique to come and take you to your future quarters. We shall see each other again soon. May the Lord bless you. I will pray for your late husband tonight and thank Him for sending you our way." With that, Catherine de Montaigne walked away, leaving nothing but the lingering sound of her footsteps as she went to take care of other matters.

Sitting before the fire, Anne de Fermont was alone once again. She rose from her chair and kneeled before the flames. Her eyes straying to the Virgin above the hearth, she stared. After a moment she closed her eyes and clasped her hands together, holding them in front of her mouth. In silence she prayed for her husband, for her life as a woman of *Nouvelle France,* and for the congregation she was to join. Uttering a single *merci,* she began to cry.

Discussion Questions

1) What is the reason that the nuns Anne meets are dressed in habits? Must nuns dress this way today? Are there other religions in which women wear similar garments?

2) What does Anne mean when she tells the first nun, "I am not like you or the other sisters. I have been married—happily"?

3) Who were the *filles du roi*? Find out how many Quebecers can trace their ancestry to them.

4) Why does the mother superior say that behind these "stone walls it is easy for me to forget the well-known strength of body and character of the women of our *Nouvelle France*"?

5) What kind of life can Anne expect in the Ursuline convent?

NATALYA AND SOFIA

Andrea Abbott

April 9, 1866

My dearest sister Sofia,

I am very excited that you are only a day's travel from home. To know that you are visiting our dear friend Anna in St. Petersburg while on a break from school in France makes the pain of our separation slightly more bearable.

My yearning to join you in St. Petersburg and visit Anna at the Nadezhdin Obstetric Institute remains unheard by the unsympathetic ears of our parents. I may as well be speaking to great-grandfather's bearded face hanging on Papa's office wall. Despite the excitement surrounding my approaching marriage, I have begun to feel trapped within the walls of our house.

I know you will think me foolish, Sofia, but as I glance up at the portraits of our ancestors, I feel just as I imagine they must have felt. Alone and caught in the elaborate metalwork that holds their frowning faces. They stare down with stern disapproval as I write these words to you. It seems that I shall remain sealed in our house as the preparations for my marriage continue.

I want you to know that your last letter snatched the breath from my chest. I cannot believe that the few midwifery students of noble descent and city origin want to hear the tales Nadya, our childhood nanny, used to tell us. I suppose a peasant village and its ways are as exotic to them as your boarding school in France and the smoky factories in Moscow are to me. I look forward to retelling stories based on the ones Nadya shared with us. It also pleases me to think of you reading them in your rich voice to the girls once this letter arrives.

I feel immense pressure trying to do justice to Nadya's stories. "Natalya," you would say, "stop exaggerating. A stone is not a mountain and a pond is not Lake Baikal." However, I am truly nervous, and my pen hovers above the paper, as I am uncertain where to begin.

Can you still picture Nadya as clearly as I can? The hardened hands. Her chapped lips softened by the laughter that always played about in her eyes. Of all the peasant souls who worked for our mother, she was the only one we knew well.

I often wonder if we would have known anything at all about the life of our peasants had she not been widowed and become our nanny. Imagine all the missed stories if she had not remained with us for those many years after we were passed on to a governess who taught us our letters.

Nadya was taken away from us by the great reforms of 1861, which are still making their uncertain and blundering way through our country. Remember Papa's bellowing laugh as he assured us not to worry, explaining that very few peasants would leave? "They may have freedom, but they still do not have land." Yet some did leave. They searched for factory jobs and opportunities in the city to earn the money to pay their debts to Papa.

When Nadya obtained her passport from the village commune and disappeared from our lives, so did our window into a world she brought to life with her words. Her stories were wrapped in the mystery that always accompanies the unfamiliar. It was a place so different from our own.

What follows, dear sister, will not illustrate the lives of the nobility dressed in the latest of French fashion but of peasants clad in their homespun garb. I hope your friends do not expect some romance set in high society. There is no way I could fill these pages with a drama set in that world. It would be full of errors, assumptions, and make-believe. Despite our family's noble name, high society is not a world which we know well.

A story is guaranteed to be captivating if it is first told beside the communal well in the village. It is from this tradition that I begin my recollections of Nadya's stories.

"Had wells but ears and tongues, not all the water they contain would put out the fire."

Vassa often lingered longer than necessary by the well, delaying the return to her *izba*. Her hands busy with work. Her ears even busier listening. Yet today she remained in the darkness of her family's home. She knew the big news would cause all the women to loiter at the well longer today than most mornings. The usual gossip would be ignored by the quick tongues.

Vassa could picture with utmost clarity how the village women would slow their usually efficient work as they spoke. Their necks would crane to catch the low, murmured voices swirling about the well. Vassa had already heard the words the avid listeners were straining to hear. She bit down to suppress the tears threatening to creep along her cheeks. The sharp, bitter taste of blood flowed across her tongue.

Just the night before, Vassa's heart had quickened with nervousness as the sun made its early descent toward the crowns of the pine trees, a sign of the approaching winter. She reached up to light the splinter hanging from the ceiling beam, thinking of the long road she had travelled to reach her upcoming marriage. First the search for a husband from within her own community followed by the quest for consent from both parents. As winter approached, the preparations became hurried, as no marriage could occur until after Easter once Lent began.

As the fragile light of the splinter began to fill the izba, her father's voice pierced the silence. "Vassa, join me here, for there is a matter we must discuss." He motioned toward the bench on which he slept. A direct man, he began before Vassa reached him. "Do you know an Anton from the village? A friend of yours, perhaps?"

"No good friend of mine, Father—just a familiar face among the villagers," she replied with a confused shake of her head.

Father nodded gravely. "You are right that he is no friend. And I pray that you speak the truth when you say he is no more than a familiar face."

"Why, Father, what has he done?"

"It is not what he has done, Vassa, but what you have done. Your previously unblemished reputation is no more. God frowns upon our entire family now, Vassa. Your pristine chastity and the entire family's honour are now under question."

Bile rose in Vassa as she sputtered out, "Wha . . . no . . . why . . . how?"

Her father's hard face blurred as tears began to leak from Vassa's terrified eyes. He continued with no reaction to her apparent despair. "If these accusations are not true, if they are evil lies, the prankster will be dealt with most harshly." Vassa was still as he continued, "So we shall wait to see if this dark cloud you have brought over our home shall lift or remain to darken our home."

Vassa knew these words were meant to give comfort. However, her anguish only deepened as she noticed her father's hasty retreat from the bench and his reluctance to even glance her way. She would have to wait for an inspection before her own family would acknowledge her.

Wait she did—first in tears and then, as the night progressed, in utter stillness and silence. When Vassa's bloodshot eyes could make out the clouds her breath formed against the steel-grey morning light, she knew the waiting was finally done.

"Lie down, knees bent," were the curt instructions of one of the three women appointed by the village elders and household heads. They lifted her skirt and began their inspection. Not a word was said as the wrinkled, cold hands conducted their search. There was not a sound even as the three hunched backs ducked quickly from the izba. Not until the echoes of their footsteps were gone did a sound somewhere between a sob and gut-wrenching laugh tear from Vassa's clenched, bloodless lips. Her betrothal, so certain mere hours before, was now rife with cracks and fraying edges.

Vassa stayed inside, shivering under her shawl. Despite the inspection meant to protect her from such violent falsehoods, she felt naked and ruined. The sun rose along a shallow arc as the village commune heard the results of the inspection. Cold winter winds sheared the clouds as the village commune associate ran from house to house spreading the verdict. The gossipers by the well gradually dispersed into the folds of daily life.

Vassa hid her shaking hand behind her shawl as she made her way to the well the next morning. The air was sharp and clear as she reached the tightly huddled backs of the village women and looked up to meet their eyes. "Did you hear?" she asked, her still, pale lips carving a smile beneath the dark circles of her dull eyes. "Perhaps you heard the news. That fool of a man, guilty of slander, has been sent to the district centre for birching. Such a pity no one trusted a girl." As she strode back toward her family's izba, head held high, a spark of light returned to her eyes.

And so, Sofia, what do you think? Oh, I do hope you believe I did justice to one of our favourite stories. Even if you decide it is too horrid to read aloud, I am glad I have written it here. Nadya's stories always provide me with the deepest of comfort. They are as constant as the cold of winter.

On another note, dear sister, to prepare you for your return home, I must admit that the household has been quite tense of late. Papa has been in one of his silent, brooding moods ever since that mad student Dmitrii Karakozov attempted to assassinate our emperor. Mama is no better.

She was in an absolute uproar to think that you were in the very same city when the gun was fired. One would think from their dark emotional state that it was one of their own children who was almost shot. Do you remember their reaction to the peasant riots and mysterious fires in St. Petersburg in 1862? Well, the tumult is now worse than what was caused by those tragic events.

I do hope your arrival home will brighten the mood considerably. You so greatly deserve your visit in St. Petersburg after your studies in France, but I want you home and close to me as my wedding day approaches. I am also quite eager for news of Anna.

With love,

Natalya

April 16, 1866

Dearest Natalya,

I cannot thank you enough for the story you wrote. The girls here adored it, and they are all eager for more. Perhaps you could continue sending the stories to Anna once my visit comes to an end.

Anna sends her regards and is saddened you were unable to join us in St. Petersburg on my visit. She is quite well, although her cough has gotten worse. I find it intriguing that Anna and many of the midwives in training are not planning to return to the countryside. Even though many of the students are peasants, they have grown attached to the ways of the city. This profession seems to give these women an escape from the restrictions of traditional life, whether they are noblewomen, peasants, or Jews hoping to live outside the Pale of Settlement.

I am grateful for the story you so artfully penned, yet you neglected to tell me news of our siblings. All the fields and factories that separate us do not make me forget how infuriating you are at times! How are the young ones? Is Ivan still climbing trees and faithfully gathering a collection of bruises and scrapes?

How is dear Maria? You must remind her that after years of waiting, two weeks is not too long a time before entering womanhood. Can't you imagine her, 16 and radiant as she becomes a part of the evenings spent in the warm, glowing parlour? I cannot believe it was only a year ago that I was in her very shoes. I remember so vividly the restlessness I felt as I waited. I acted like a young girl. Soon, though, she will enter our world of womanhood, and the task of finding a husband will begin in earnest.

Other than a few colourful metaphors, you also neglected to tell me how you are. I know that after my departure more responsibilities fell to you, such as helping Mother tend to the ill peasants and managing the property. With your upcoming marriage, this must be a lot to handle. Please remember you are my most cherished sister and you can always confide in me.

Yours always,

Sofia

April 28, 1866

Dear Sofia,

I see that I can still inspire frustration even through a letter. I am sorry for neglecting to include much family news. I was called away to help prepare the little ones for their after-supper inspection by Mother. As you know well, this is always followed by evening prayers. Grandmother was dictating them that night, and you know how picky she is about clean hands and spotless clothing.

You are right about Ivan. He had a bruise in the shape of a heart of which he was particularly proud. As for Maria, she has become my shadow, and my patience is beginning to run thin. Actually, I dare say shadow is too kind a word, for at least shadows do not shower you with constant queries.

I know I should be more like you, yet despite my greatest efforts, I cannot always rein in my impatience. At the news of your return home, all our sisters (except Maria) have momentarily forgotten their dreams of marriage and have begun to pester Mama about joining you at boarding school in France. None wants to attend finishing school in Moscow or St. Petersburg. Yet, despite their collective desire to join you in France, everyone loves the new tutor.

I find it so distressing that she has never been married. Can you fathom the idea, dear Sofia? If I were to remain unmarried, I would feel like such a heavy burden to the family.

Anna was once married before she moved to St. Petersburg. Although her training has put a hold on the idea of a second husband, I do know the search is uppermost in her parents' thoughts. I hope they will find one with a strong constitution, for I do not want her to go through the grief of losing a second husband to tuberculosis.

This thought leads me naturally to your next inquiry. It is true that doubts are beginning to form cracks in the strong front I have so carefully crafted. I want to begin by telling you that I really am thankful for my upcoming marriage. I do relish the idea of finally leaving home. I can rest easy knowing that my future children and I will be well cared for by Alexander. I must admit, it is also pleasing to my long-suffering ego that I will be moving up in the world. But Sofia! Oh, the panic and fear I feel in the dark-hidden crevices of my heart.

I know my marriage to Alexander makes Papa and Mama smile, but I have only met him a handful of times. I will most likely carry more than 10 of his children, and although I fancy myself in love, he is still a stranger to me. Am I being ridiculous, dear sister? I do know that these silly doubts are of no real importance. I will go forward with the marriage. Before I know it, we will both be stooped over and wrinkled, reminiscing by the fireplace.

Tell Anna I will be sure to send her a letter with another story about Vassa.

Your faithful sister,

Natalya

P.S. Please do hurry home. I need my sister by my side.

Discussion Questions

1) Why does Natalya say that the ancestors in the pictures would disapprove of her?

2) Sofia reminds Natalya about the peasant woman Nadya and the stories she told them when they were children. What does it tell us about Sofia and Natalya's family that they had a peasant woman working for them?

3) In the story told by Natalya, why are the village women checking under Vassa's skirts? What does this tell us about the qualities of women valued in Vassa's village?

4) What does it tell us of Sofia and Natalya that Vassa's story is one of their favourites?

5) Use the internet and try to figure out what became of each of the people in this story.

Melissa Aytenfisu is a Canadian artist who concentrates in oil paintings, digital print media, photography, printmaking, and drawing. A native of Edmonton, she earned a bachelor's degree in education before moving to Montreal, where she eventually received a Bachelor of Fine Arts degree from Concordia University. During the years in between, Aytenfisu taught high school in Quebec and China while honing her craft and creating works that have appeared in exhibitions across multiple continents. Her experiences growing up in a multiracial family of nine and travelling through Africa, Asia, and North America have directed her artistic practice toward themes of identity, mobility, social justice, and the human body in motion.

Nathan M. Greenfield has been a college professor for more than 25 years. He is a regular contributor to the *Times Literary Supplement* and the principal author of *Adventures in World History* (Emond Montgomery), the textbook used in Ontario's Grade 12 history course. As well, he is the author of four military histories, including *The Damned: The Canadians at the Battle of Hong Kong and the POW Experience,* which was shortlisted for the Governor General's Award for Non-Fiction in 2010, and *The Forgotten: Canadian POWs, Escapers and Evaders in Europe, 1941-45,* both published by Harper Collins, Canada.

John Connolly has taught in Canada, Papua New Guinea, and Mali. He has also been involved in education as a school board trustee/chair. As well, he worked on social development issues for many years with the Government of Canada and is currently focused on clean water and sanitation issues in the international context. With Storyteller Documentary Films, he produced a video about perception.